CHRISTIE

Puffin Books
Editor : Kaye Webb
The Cold Flame

Five-and-twenty years the soldier went fighting for
the king. Five-and-twenty years, five-and-twenty
wounds; and at the end of it the king gave him just
one silver dollar for his services.

So the soldier trudged away into the witch wood,
far from the city. 'Better here in the dust of the road
and the brute sun than there in the city of men and
kings,' he thought. Deep in the wood he found a
witch, who put him to work for his keep, and he
won from her the cold blue flame she coveted, and
lit his last scrap of tobacco in it.

Then in the smoke appeared a little manikin,
black and naked, bowing before him. 'I am at your
command,' it said. 'As master of the flame, you have
it in your power to summon me, and I cannot
refuse.'

So then the soldier went back to the city of men
to try his new power and teach the callous king a
lesson.

James Reeves has enlarged on this old story from
Grimm's Fairy Tales to make a wonderfully
memorable, moving, and sometimes sinister tale,
suitable for all readers who feel themselves too old
for the simpler versions of fairy tales they used to
love.

Cover design by Charles Keeping

James Reeves

The Cold Flame

Illustrated by Charles Keeping

Penguin Books

Penguin Books Ltd, Harmondsworth,
Middlesex, England
Penguin Books Inc., 7110 Ambassador Road,
Baltimore, Maryland 21207, U.S.A.
Penguin Books Australia Ltd, Ringwood,
Victoria, Australia

First published by Hamish Hamilton 1967
Published in Puffin Books 1970
Copyright © James Reeves, 1967
Illustrations copyright © Charles Keeping, 1967

Made and printed in Great Britain by
Hazell Watson & Viney Ltd,
Aylesbury, Bucks
Set in Linotype Juliana

This book is sold subject to the condition that
it shall not, by way of trade or otherwise, be lent,
re-sold, hired out, or otherwise circulated without
the publisher's prior consent in any form of
binding or cover other than that in which it is
published and without a similar condition
including this condition being imposed on the
subsequent purchaser

Contents

1. *The Outrage*

The soldier dragged himself to the rickety table, lowered his body painfully on to the bench alongside. The tableboards, weathered silver, threw back the hard noon glare of the autumn sun. The three fingers of his left hand scraped from his screwed-up eyes the sweaty hair, black but for the white dust from the road.

'The end,' said the soldier and echoed his own words in a rasping sigh. 'The end.'

His knobby staff clattered on the baked earth. With a groan he picked it up and hit the door in the wall behind him. He hit three times, not hard but deliberately.

'You should make haste. I am a soldier.'

The landlord stood with legs wide apart, looking down at him.

'You are no soldier.'

'I was a soldier.'

'You have neither musket, pike nor broadsword. I know a sturdy beggar when I see one.'

'I was a soldier.'

'You have nothing of the soldier but authority, and nothing of a beggar but this cudgel.'

'I need food. Food and drink. I can pay.'

'I am something of a scholar, albeit the host of a poor ale-house. Yet I need small learning to tell me the weight of your purse.'

The soldier fumbled in his belt, drew out a silver piece and threw it on the table.

'I will eat and drink as much as that will buy.'

'My wife is a she-devil. This is devil's country, witches' country.'

'It's all my soldiering brought me. It is all you'll get.'

The landlord shoved open the door and went in, presently returning with a steaming dish and a horn spoon.

'Rabbit stew,' he said. 'I have Rhine wine.'

'No wine,' said the soldier. 'Bring me all the beer my money will pay for. That and this stew.'

The sight of a fairish flagon of cool beer and the good smell of the stew drove something of the strain from the soldier's screwed-up face.

'Times are bad,' the landlord said. 'My wife is a she-devil.'

'Times are bad.' The soldier took the words as an invitation to talk. 'Five-and-twenty bad years I went soldiering for him that calls himself King. Five-and-twenty years, five-and-twenty wounds.'

'This is witch country. You come from the city?'

'From the city ruled by him who calls himself King. One month ago we parted, him and me. Begging brought me to the stocks, taking what was another's brought me to the whipping-post. That is nothing to me.'

With the three fingers and thumb of his left hand the soldier clawed the rabbit-bone he chewed from. His scarred right hand grasped the flagon.

'Now to the forest, country of demons.'

'No worse than the city, country of men. Men and kings. Five-and-twenty wounds for one silver dollar. One silver dollar for five-and-twenty years. The marching was worse than the fighting. The drilling was worse than the marching. At Leipzig I lost a finger. In Flanders I'd a ball through the knee. At Mittelhausen I lay without moving and watched the flies patrolling an open wound in my thigh. See. That was a Spanish pike.'

He lifted his hand from the flagon, drew back his torn

breeches. The landlord looked without curiosity at the livid
scar running from knee to groin.

'The billets were bad sometimes. Straw used by the horses.
Muck and flies. Bad food. Cuts aching from Saxony to
Belgium.'

'It was bad, but now you're discharged.'

'Now I'm discharged – and it was *not* bad.'

'The sun shines. It is not bad for the road.'

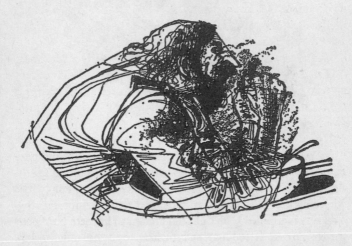

'The sun shines now – now it is too late. The summer rain
smashed the harvest. So the young men go to be soldiers, and
the old soldiers are cashiered. I'm not old, but no good for
fighting. So the captain told me. More beer.'

'You've drunk it all.'

'One silver dollar the King gave me. No pension, no
thanks. "Times," he said, "are bad. New wars, new soldiers.
You have no fight left in you." That's what he said, the one
that calls himself King. I served his father, a better man. This
young one – they call him the young one though he's nearer
fifty years than forty – is a man of flint. His eyes are steel.

Take out his eyes and strike them on his heart, and you could fire a powder-barrel. Blow up the palace, blow up his brat. "You're too old," says the drunken captain. "His Majesty's older than me," says I. "You're too old for fighting. You're too crippled to march, too broken to fire straight. Your rotten carcass is too patched to keep out the rain." More beer.'

'You've drunk all your money and more.'

'A mean landlord is worse than a bad captain, and a flint king is worse than a mean landlord. I'll be gone. Better the forest of devils than the city of kings. May the young men he got cheap because there was no harvest turn coward and give up the city of kings to the Flemings or the Dutch or the Spaniards or the Turks, for all I care. May the King be strung up on his flagpole and his brat be carried off by a company of Muscovites!'

The soldier had raised his clenched face to the blinding sun,

as if craving succour to strengthen his curse, so that he had
not noticed the fresh flagon of beer placed at his elbow by the
landlord.

'You can pay,' the landlord said, 'without silver.'

The soldier drank greedily. From his knapsack the landlord pulled a wooden pipe whose end he had spied sticking
out of the top.

'A tune on your flute will pay for all.'

The soldier, now calm, slowly wiped his mouth with the
back of his right hand, and took up the flute.

'Are you by any chance acquainted with the tune they call
"The Birdcatcher"?'

The soldier placed the pipe to his lips, stopped the holes as
best he could with seven fingers, and blew. A cracked wheeze
obliged the landlord to hide a smile.

'With this thing,' the soldier said, 'you know what goes in.
You never know what will come out.'

2. The Wood

Too old to fight. Too young to die. Too young to lie and rot
on the heathland beyond the city, to lie among the huddled
stones in the overgrown churchyard. Five-and-twenty years,
five-and-twenty wounds. A body too patched to keep out the
weather; legs too broken to stand and fight, to turn and run.
Too bent to stand in the palace guard, the stiff sentry-box by
the great gate. Too many second-class troops already, too
many for light duties about the palace.

'I fought and marched for him from end to end of Europe.
For him I tramped from the Baltic to the Peninsula, from
Normandy to the Alps. I smelt the pines of the Baltic, that
salt, wintry wind; the warm olive-scents of Spain. I have
smelt powder, horses, dung, sweat, blood, sour wine, garlic,
urine, hot leather, men's feet, corpses, salt wind, pines and
olives. The movement and beat is always one, the beat of
tramping boots. What makes men move, what makes them
go on, on, on, on to the end? The end, the end, the end. It is
the end. There is no end but the witch wood, the wood of
wickedness.

'But better here in the dust of the road and the brute sun
than there in the city of men and kings, flint hearts and steel
captains.

'What makes the boots go on? A fine thing, a soldier's
boot – stout sole, bright nails, supple tops, flapping and
smacking to the march of feet. What matter if the feet inside
are grimed and sweating, calloused and corned, the nails in-
grown, the instep pitted by fleas, running sores between
toes? It is the boots march on..to fight, to stand, to turn and

run, to bear the soldier to victory and defeat, into the cobbled town under the gate-arch. Tramp, tramp, the boots bear onwards the worn heart and the patched body. What animal would go the same way – on, on, to no end but a master's service? A horse would drop long before the end. An ox or a cow would die standing. Only a dead ox, his hide turned into boots, could tramp as a live man tramps. Left right left. Left right left. It is the tramping that counts, it is the marching proves the man.

'Five-and-twenty years, if they could be untramped, unmarched, unfought, where would they take me? Back to the green day when the boy set out to serve under the old king's colours. Eyes screwed against the sun to fix on the flapping colours, proud-eagled, scarlet and gold against the blazing sky over the green summer. Boys were as animals, playing at soldiers, fighting each other naked in the slippery pools, climbing the trees like cats, chasing in the fields like hares, diving like trout. Five-and-twenty springs, five-and-twenty winters.'

Oxen in the lanes, cows in the fields, the town curs snarling at his heels. City and country were gone. Only the road in front – the road and the wolfwood, the place of witches.

Listening now to only his feet in their patched, broken boots, the soldier knew that never again would the beat be sturdy and regular as when they marched over the plains of Flanders, the plains of Hungary. Steady and firm, that sound had been the bass to all the sounds of his life as a man. Now the note came shuffling and syncopated, like the sound of an old, spent clock. It was the limp of worn feet, worn boots bearing a spent body. He did not hate the town curs, the dung-caked flanks of the oxen blocking the lanes outside the city : he hated the dead rabbit, chewed and digesting inside his scarred belly. He hated the food and the beer that had cost

him the dollar he had sold his pride for. One silver dollar, one hundred pennies, fourpence a year for saving the young flint king and his old dead father. Better to have sent the coin spinning into the flint, arrogant face. It would have been prison, a hanging most likely. But he had eaten and drunk his pride, and now it sickened him.

The boots dragged on, not grumbling.

Five-and-twenty summers, unmarched, unrolled like an old trooper's windy tale in a hedge-inn's corner – what sounds would they bring? Trumpets in the drenched mornings; kettle-drums; laughter and swearing of raw-voiced youngsters; rumbling and growling of veterans; the neigh of horses; bells in pious hill villages; bells from town steeples and huzzas for relieving soldiers; carters' oaths; singing of milkmaids; commands of stablelads to whinnying horses; barking of dogs, cackle of hens, squealing of pigs, screaming of cocks in an endless line like beacons of sound over counties, countries, nations. Rolling of thunder, rolling of cannon, hooves of cavalry on wooden bridges; jaunty sharp tunes of fifes; familiar bawdy songs, and the groans of wounded men, groans of the dying; whining of children and sobs of the inconsolable. Under it all, unrolled from the five-and-twenty years, was the beat of boots. Left, left, left right left. Soldiers must curse and sing; women must rail and weep; animals scream and brawl. The march must go on, endlessly nearing an end.

Under the trees it was cooler, though the air was close. On the needle-strewn forest floor the limping feet dragged softer. The sun slanted more nearly level through the ranked pine-trunks. A creature chattered now and again and was still. This was the wood of witches, the wood of outlaws. The soldier had heard tell of outlaws. Perhaps he would find them. Perhaps he would not find them and die, and the crows would fall upon and tear at his scarred carcass. He had no food, no money, not much strength except the strength of habit, the strength in his patched, broken boots.

To the soldier, as to all at that time and in that country, if they were alone, nightfall brought fear. Fear in a wood at nightfall can be a huge, overwhelming thing. Then from the past of a people, the ignorant deeps beyond consciousness, undefined, evil forces assemble and crowd. But weariness is the foe of fear. Despair is the ally of courage. Sense overcomes ignorance, and imagination drowses. He who has struck down the Turk has nothing to fear from demons.

A wind passed, arousing the soldier from the indifference to the coming of dark. He tightened his grip on the knapsack, and quickened his pace a fraction.

'I will go on till I can see no more,' he said to himself quietly, 'then I will lie down wherever I am. If the wolves find me, they will make a poor supper.'

Then he raised his voice in defiance and shouted :

'Wolves and devils, do your worst ! Goblins and hob-goblins, molest me at your peril. He who was the King's soldier greets you and spurns you. Do your worst, do you hear ! Do your worst, your worst, I say !'

There was no answer, except perhaps a light movement high up among the pines, as a shiver of autumn passed.

The soldier shuffled on. The sun had sunk out of sight, and darkness came in strides. Here and there a creature rustled or pattered over the floor of the forest. An owl hooted, answered by another, far off.

The soldier trudged on, in what direction he had no idea.

Five-and-twenty years. ... Five-and-twenty paces. After five-and-twenty paces, he would lie down under a tree and move no further.

Left right left. Left right left. At the tenth pace he raised his eyes in the direction of what seemed a faint glow or gleam among the trees to his left. He changed his direction and stumbled towards the light. A tree root tripped him. He felt for the trunks with his knobbed staff. The light grew brighter, though not welcoming, as he neared it. It was a pale light, not warm, almost green in its coldness. The trees thinned to a clearing. As he crossed it, a dog began to howl.

3. *The Woman*

'Down, Kaiser. Down, I say!'

A bass voice grated, as the dog's howl rose in answer to the soldier's repeated blow on the door with the knob of his staff.

'Down, cur!'

The scrape of bolts. The dog's howl subsided to a restless whimper.

The soldier stumbled in, almost falling against the figure outlined by the pale, greenish light. Despite the voice, it was a woman. The mongrel cur, spurned by its mistress's foot, slunk into a corner out of sight, whimpering.

'Shelter for the night,' the soldier demanded. 'Shelter and food.'

'Give up your cudgel, soldier. It will do you no good.'

The woman clutched his staff. He gave it up without protest. Then, bereft of its support, he sank to the bench under the window, still holding his knapsack. He dropped his head into his hands, elbows supported by the edge of a bare wooden table.

'You break in upon urgent work. The wise woman is at work. Do you not see?'

The soldier raised his head a little, groaning with weariness, but was aware only of the source of the light he had first seen through the small, square, cobwebbed window in the wall behind him. On the spikes of a branched candlestick of black iron, three fat candles burned with a sickly light. A grey cat had sprung on to the table at the soldier's entrance, and now stood in front of him, back arched, spitting.

'Down, Venus – down, my beauty! Come, then.'

The bass voice wheedled low. A hand came from under a black shawl, gathered the grey thin animal, set it down on the floor. Becoming accustomed to the light, the soldier looked at the woman. She was no mumbling crone, like the witches he had been brought up to believe in, the ancient, wrecked creatures pointed out to him for wise women when he was a boy. She was almost young, handsomely built, with strong hands and knotted, shapely wrists. Her face was in shadow, but the eyes glinted piercingly in the sickly glare. She was draped, rather than clothed, in a dark, striped skirt, a black shawl over her shoulders, a black scarf over her head. Strands of hair escaped from the scarf and fell about her eyes – startlingly light hair, pale, almost ashen gold.

'I am no soldier. All I need is shelter – shelter and food.'

'A soldier you were. The wise woman will give shelter and food.'

She moved to the farther end of the table, where evidently she had been at work, sat down on a stool, stared at him with a look made half of contempt and half of granite indifference. He could see her more clearly now. He was aware of a straight, prominent nose, full red lips, but most of all, the needle-sharp black crystal eyes where, if there was any colour, the light was too feeble to show it.

The mongrel snuffled sulkily in a corner; the cat scratched at the door.

'What is it, my beauty? Has a rat come to call? Did she hear a rat, then, my sweet Venus?'

In three swift strides the woman reached the door, let the cat out into the night.

'The wise woman sends her on errands. Venus works in the night.'

Silently she swooped across the room to a cupboard in the corner, brought out a bowl, a cracked dish, horn spoon, mug of dull tinware.

'You may well look at me,' the woman said. 'These eyes can do me good service. There's not many dare look at me if they have done me wrong. I planted my nine toads nine year agone, and they have given me what you call the evil eye.'

The soldier shrank involuntarily from the food he was about to take from the bowl, a kind of porridge, cold but not unsavoury to look at.

'There is no evil in the bowl. Nor in the mug, though the ale be soured a little by the sun's heat. Here is bread too. But I must be paid.'

She put on the cracked dish a hunk of grey bread.

'Here is pig's grease, but not for eating.'

She rubbed ointment from a box on the lids of her eyes, the palms of her hands. The soldier became conscious of the odours he had been too weary to remark on his first entrance into the hovel. The air was musty, tainted with animal smells, smells of decay, herbs drying, burnt tallow. A nasty place he had come to, a place to turn the stomach even of an old campaigner.

'It will be paid – the score will be paid.'

He desired suddenly to be out in the fresh air of the forest. He felt stifled. But he was weary still, and hungry. He must eat and rest. The noise of boots had almost died in his head, leaving it hot and aching. The infinite trudging of his soldier years was now only a dull memory, like the feeling of a tooth that has ceased to ache. Disgust struggled in him with sloth, a great yawning desire that everything should end.

The food and the ale, poor though they were, revived his consciousness, if not his spirits, drove off the numbness he wished would increase. He became aware of objects piled on the floor, strewn in corners, hung from rusted nails in the rafters of the low, smoke-charred ceiling. A hedgehog, dead and shrivelled, the skin of a weasel, forked roots, a random assortment of clothing, the skeleton of a rabbit or a hare, a hollow gourd or pumpkin, bunches of drying herbs, a horse's skull, a wooden bowl filled with what seemed to be teeth, part of a leather harness, green with mould, cracked and twisted from age.

The soldier looked at the woman. Oblivious of him now, she was on the stool at the far end of the table, whispering, crooning, mouthing incomprehensible words and phrases. What she was making with her strong, active fingers looked like a doll. Skeins of straw were tied tightly, dividing half-way down in the likeness of a pair of legs. Straw arms stuck out near the top. The whole image was surmounted by a withered apple, hollowed out with a knife, and into the hole was wedged the doll's neck. On top of the apple the woman had stuck strands of red hair, perhaps from a human being, perhaps from some animal. A square of torn red cloth pinned to the shoulders served to suggest a cloak. Eyes and mouth had been gouged out of the apple-head. This grotesque semblance of a man was perhaps no more than a foot high.

'Rich he is,' murmured the woman, half to herself, half to the soldier, quietly in her bass voice, in a tone of almost loving malice. 'Rich and powerful. I know his name but may not name him. Born in an evil day to wreck and ruin mine and me. Out in the road he flung us, pressing my husband into the mines. Yes, I was married; the wise woman had her man. Seven years my man has rotted in the mines, in the dark and the wet. They called him a witch when a foaling horse he had looked on miscarried, and the harvest was blighted with the mildew.'

She picked up the doll from the table and fixed upon it her brilliant eyes with a concentration of malice that seemed to burn into its tightly knotted straw.

'Rich you are and sinful, fat with all greed and wickedness. Not for long will you roll in your coach and bring misery on

poor householders. You shall be racked with cramps, twisted
with pain, burning with fevers, rotted –'

The voice grew more powerful and more menacing, its deep
tones screwed up to a falsetto. She stopped suddenly, addressed the soldier.

'Can you write, handle a pen?'

Wearily the soldier assented. She gave him a quill from an
owl's wing, a scrap of yellowed paper, dark fluid in a horn.

'Write,' she ordered. 'Write this.

> 'Slow shalt thou rot.
> Cramps in thy limbs,
> Hot coals in thy belly,
> Pains in thy head,
> Thy breast and thy members.
> I do wish this with all my heart,
> With all my strength.
> Slow may thou rot.'

She finished with triumphant malevolence, sprang from
her stool, took from a shelf a twisted paper. The soldier, no
skilled writer, had found it hard to keep pace with her curse.
No sooner had the quill scratched its way to the final words
than she seized the document from him, scattered upon it the
contents of her twist of paper, folded it across, once, twice,
three times.

'Dried with dust from his house-floor,' she said, and took
from a fold in her shawl an old horn comb from which already
most of the teeth were missing. She broke from it seven of the
remaining teeth and with her right hand savagely stabbed
them into the image of her enemy. Two she drove into the
eyes, two into the belly. With two she impaled the folded
paper on which the soldier had scratched her curse, transfix-
ing it to the doll's breast. The seventh with a demoniac scream
she drove through the paper into the heart.

'There, there, and there!'

'What will you do? Bury him?'

'No.'

'Burn him then?'

'No. He must be long in dying. I may tie him to a tree, so that the wind and weather rot him slowly. I may fix him to the root of a willow overhanging the stream, so that the water brings lingering ruin. I will seek counsel of my sisters.'

The woman placed the image on top of the cupboard in the corner.

'This should I have performed in secret, but the soldier will not talk. I have power over him. If he talks, he will be sorry.'

The soldier, who had finished eating, roused himself from the fascinated horror induced by the witch.

'I can keep counsel. Now I must rest.'

'You may sleep in my house,' the woman said with a sudden sly wheedling in her voice.

She made as if to draw apart the folds of her shawl. In horror and loathing the soldier stood up and stumbled towards the door.

'I am weary. I will lie down outside, under the trees.'

'If the soldier will, he may bed in the straw of the shed, where my dog sleeps. Come, Kaiser, take the gentleman to your bed. Tomorrow the soldier shall pay for food and shelter. He shall dig the garden. It must be ready by All-hallows to plant seeds – seeds of henbane, wolfsbane, ragwort, nightshade. Tomorrow you shall fork my garden. I shall seek counsel of my sisters.'

4. The Earth

Driving his spade into the black earth, the soldier remembered a party of his comrades in Brabant, a dozen years ago, forced to dig their own graves. There they would be slaughtered by the enemy, laid in the shallow pits, covered hastily by the pioneers. They had done the work slowly, laboriously, with a ritual thoroughness that had seemed strange yet not to be wondered at. The last office they would perform for themselves or anyone else, a job to be done well for the job's sake. He turned the soil, buried the weeds. Spit after spit, row after row, he toiled for the toil's sake. Half-naked in the noonday sun of the hot autumn, he toiled on. It was as if he dug his own grave. He thought of his comrades, comrades of five-and-twenty years, buried in haste in the rich soil of the Low Countries, the chalk soil of the hills, the clay soil of the valleys, the hard, unyielding soil of the forests. His shirt cast off for the heat, he worked only in breeches and boots. Sweat poured down the furrows of his scars, dripped from his armpits, slid down his forearms, his wrists, his good right hand, his maimed left hand. He was forced to wipe the handle of the spade on a bunch of rank grass to prevent it from slipping. Yet the dull rhythm of the task brought a kind of peace, the peace of dogged despair, the peace of death.

'My grave,' he thought. 'The end – this is the end.'

If it was his grave, it would be a refuge from the woman, a refuge from which even she, with her unearthly power, could not draw him. The night had been restless, small creatures rustling in the straw, leaves complaining in the night wind.

He had turned and moved in his half sleep, too weary for the oblivion of unconsciousness. Towards dawn he had slept, only to awaken at cock-crow, stiff and aching. He was aware of a griping pain in his belly, a gnawing taste of sourness in his mouth. But it was his spirit, not his flesh, that sickened. The other side of the wall, in the woman's dwelling, there was evil and malice. A man must be starving to take bread from her. He had known women from early manhood and throughout his days of campaigning. He had never thought of them as anything but a comfort to the spirit and the body, an unlooked-for haven in the restless voyage, the unending march of the campaigner. This woman was different, one to turn victuals to dust, drink to poison, a man to a swine.

The cock crew again, far off and desolate. The soldier rose, resolute only to escape, to run to the outlaws or to death, whichever he met first. In the grey light he picked up his knapsack, felt for his boots. They were not to be found. Supposing he had, in his exhaustion, left them behind in the hovel before going out to bed in the straw; he made towards the door, determined to bang his way inside and retrieve the boots. Without them his life was suspended; with them he could resume the endless trudge.

Startled to hear a voice, he withheld the hand that reached for the latch. A mindless, meaningless chattering, harsh and shrill, broke the silence of dawn. With surprise but without fear he discerned a bird perched on an iron bar let into the wall beside the door. It was a magpie, chained by its foot so that it could only hop and flutter, or dip its beak into the iron cup that hung on the bar. The voice spoke no word, but uttered the sounds of cursing and alarm.

'Poor bird,' the soldier said softly, raising his hand to stroke the feathers with the back of a crooked forefinger. The magpie turned its head and jabbed at him with its beak. The latch

clicked. The door opened, and the woman stood before him, smiling.

'Is the soldier ready for work? Has he come for his boots?'

He followed her in, sat down on the bench where he had rested the evening before, began to don his boots.

The gruel she gave him was thin and salt. He drank it without relish, swallowing down the loathing he felt for her and her ways.

'To gain power over a man or a woman, possess yourself of his clothes – gloves, kerchief, boots. Bury a shoe in the ground, and no matter how healthy the owner, he will shrivel and pine. But my soldier must be strong and well. Take the spade and dig.'

Hour after hour he dug, turning the black earth, burying the weeds, casting the flints and chalk on a heap against the hedge. No wind, no clouds, only the hot sun rising higher towards noon. So he must pay for his food, his night's lodging. Birds came from the wood and inspected the soldier, scratched for worms in the soil he had turned. They seemed to him to be without gratitude, but he was glad to serve them. So he had been served by poor cottagers and labourers through whose countries he had marched. They owed him nothing. They gave freely of what little they had – poor bread, stale beer, sour milk. Now he was repaying the creatures of the air as he repaid the woman to whom he owed the life he did not desire.

The day wore on, the sun declined, an evening breeze cooled his sweating body. His scars ached. Blisters burned even on his hardened hands. At supper he gazed intently at the woman as she sat opposite him, plying her evil tasks. Pity flowed into his heart – pity that any human creature could be so contemptible. She had done nothing but relieve his wants and ply her trade. But she was evil, doomed to do evil, offspring of the devil. Others had suffered as she had, but had survived without malice.

'Tomorrow before breakfast you shall finish the digging. Then you must pay for tonight's lodging with another day's work. There is the woodshed to be filled, for winter will come, and I shall be cold.'

The soldier said nothing, his jaws moving over his victuals. If she could work such evil, could he not use her power? But he had nothing belonging to the man who called himself King – not a shoe, not a glove, not a hair. Perhaps there were other ways.

'I have dug for you,' he said at last. 'I will finish the digging. I will cut wood for you. I am a man who pays for all. I am a soldier and have fought for honour. I have fought for the King. He owes more than you. He gave me a silver piece. You have given me life.'

'Where is the silver piece?'

A gleam, a smile came into the woman's eyes, and she spoke in wheedling tones.

'It is spent.'

'A pity. I could have used it. The King can be destroyed.'

It was as if she read his mind.

'No.'

'My sisters in Britain called up spirits against the foul King of the Scots who sought to destroy them. They sent him pains, cramps, toothache; they whistled up winds to wreck the ship that carried him. Even a king is no match for wise women.'

'Vengeance belongs to the Lord. Vengeance is not of the Evil One.'

The woman shrugged her white shoulders which gleamed in the greenish light from the candles. The black shawl had slipped loose; the shoulders were bare but for the strands of pale gold hair hanging over them.

'As the soldier wishes. Come, Venus, out with you.'

The cat slipped from her lap, stood mewing at the door. The woman let the cat out, and the soldier followed to his solitary bed of straw. He slept soundly. His mind was at rest, dreamless and out of reach of the cries of owls, the barking of foxes.

5. *The Well*

'We be soldiers three,
    Pardonna-moy, je vous en prie,
Lately come out of the Low Countree,
    With never a penny of money.'

In his rough, dry voice the soldier chanted the old song under his breath, slowly, rhythmically, to the sound of the chopping. The digging finished, he had thrown aside his spade and taken up the axe with relief. It was a man's work, splitting wood, when all was said. It was better than splitting heads. He could fancy each log was his enemy, this great knotty piece of elm the King. One silver dollar for five-and-twenty years. Someone had already cut the wood into thick logs – an outlaw, the woman had said, passing that way and needing food.

'But he cheated me. I pursued him with curse and ill omen. They say that he dwindled and died. It is better not to cross the wise woman.'

The pile of logs lessened slowly, the pile of split faggots increased in the woodshed. The day grew hotter, hotter than ever autumn should be.

Through the long hot afternoon the soldier toiled, sustained only by the Devil's comforter, despair. Why work? To live. Why live? To go on trudging, to find the outlaws, to carve out a hard, bitter, dangerous living outside the law, outside the unjust, heartless laws. What were the laws? Lawyers' lies to keep in power him who called himself King. Better to live with the outlaws, living hard, sleeping well.

Slowly the wood-pile grew. Obedient to the will, the naked

will of despair, the axe rose and fell, regularly, unvaryingly, yet not without malice, not without a mindless, venomous brutality. It was as if the axe was animal, relentless, savage, biting its way into the harmless grain of the wood to wreak some half-articulate vengeance in the soul of the wielder.

> *'Here, good fellow, I drink to thee*
> *Pardonna-moy, je vois en prie,*
> *To all good fellows wherever they be*
> *With never a penny of money.'*

It was dusk when the last of the wood was chopped. It was almost night, for the day, though hot, had not been long. It was the time of bats, the time when bats squeak and swoop through the warm darkness.

'You must pass one more night with the wise woman. It is too late to fare further tonight. The soldier would be slain by wolves or stray from the path and lose footing in the bog.'

'Can I reach the outlaws tomorrow? Will you show me the way?'

'One of them did me wrong. I sent him to the devil. Tonight let the pretty soldier stay with the woman. Come, let me give the soldier his supper.'

'It is too hot. I had rather sleep out.'

Crooked and malicious, the woman peered at the soldier from under her dishevelled hair.

'Better to be within. Perhaps there will be a storm.'

'Will it be you who conjures it up?'

'I or my sisters. But I say nothing. The judges are wicked. If there is a storm, perhaps some great person will perish. To-morrow I will show you the way. But first you must do one more task, to pay for this night's lodging. It is a light task. It will take little time.'

'What is the task?'

The woman's bass voice became intense, urgent.

'I have lost something precious to me, something of great and powerful strength. The soldier must go down the well and bring up the blue flame.'

'The blue flame?'

'It is my servant. I let it fall down the dry well. The soldier must get it back: I cannot do it by myself.'

'I'll meddle with no such things.'

But even as he spoke, in weariness and despair, he was conscious of the woman's dark will.

'The soldier will bring the blue flame from the well. Then he may go. To bed now, pretty soldier.'

Under the trees it was cooler than indoors, and the heaps of pine needles were soft enough. Yet he felt stifled. The bats had swooped to rest, hanging upside down in the shed and under the trees. Owls cried murderously. Little creatures squeaked and shuffled in the undergrowth. Nothing was at rest. All nature seemed possessed of a spirit of uneasiness and foreboding. The soldier dropped into a fitful sleep. He dreamed in snatches, woke continually, felt for his knapsack, his cudgel and his boots, which lay beside him.

Why not wait till first light and steal away from the place of bad omen? But the soldier had strength only to resist the woman's assaults upon him, none to withstand her malice and revengefulness.

He dreamed that he was in the presence of the King, who held an axe. Behind the King stood his pale daughter, the eighteen-year-old princess soon to marry a foreign count, so it was said. Around the King hovered the witch, grinning and grimacing with evil delight. Drawn by her power, the soldier came into the presence of the King. The King raised his axe; there was a peal of insane laughter; the soldier awoke, drenched to the skin. A night bird was laughing hysterically. All around were the scufflings of little padded feet, the squeaks and snufflings of creatures in commotion. The soldier thought at first that he had broken out in a sweat at the climax of a fever. But what drenched his shirt, his breeches and his body was rain. It fell through the trees in heavy drops. Thunder rolled, growing ever nearer. Forked lightning flashed in the patches of sky between the tree-tops. The ground beneath a tree was no place to stay in a storm. The soldier picked up his things and groped towards the shed where he had spent the last two nights. Helped by a prolonged occurrence of lightning, he found the entrance to the shed. Lying on the straw, he counted the hours until the storm passed over and the morning came. Day – day of the final task, day of liberation.

Mechanically swallowing his breakfast gruel, the soldier

wondered what cunning the woman would have in store for him, now that she knew he must depart. He could scarcely bear to look round the hovel, so foul and malodorous were the skins of creatures, the bones and ragged, unwashed clothes, the potions and oils with which she performed her unclean practices. He looked at the woman. Her face was shut and expressionless. The mongrel Kaiser drooled and muttered over a bone, and Venus the cat licked her lean and mangy joints under her mistress's chair.

His knapsack over his shoulder, the man followed the

woman to the end of the patch of ground that separated her hovel from the deep forest. He was not going to stay a minute longer than necessary. He was not going back into her evil dwelling if he could help it. As they left the hovel, the chained magpie swore. They passed through a patch of stinging nettles, ferns and foxgloves. Presently they stopped under an alder tree. A little way further on the soldier saw the dry well, a wide, black hole in the earth lined with stones. A wheel on a rusted axle was supported over the well-mouth on two uprights of mouldering wood.

'Look down, soldier. What do you see?'

Apprehensive under his mask of calm indifference, the soldier stood on the edge of the hole and looked down.

'Nothing.'

The word sounded ominous, echoing hollowly in the deep shaft of the well.

'Look closer. You will see.'

Keeping on the farther side of the well from the woman, whom he trusted no more than he would trust one thought to be a spy in time of battle, the soldier gazed down.

As his eyes accustomed themselves to not being dazzled by the brightness of day between the trees, he made out something far down in the well. At such a depth the light was tiny and insignificant, but it was unmistakably what the woman wanted to regain.

6. The Blue Flame

A task to be done, like other tasks – a task to be finished with. Then out of the witch wood, away from the witch's house, the smell of malice and ill-will. He had not much against the woman. She had fed and housed him in her fashion. Hard usage, perhaps, had brought her to her way of life : hard usage of him had made their paths cross. Yet he was disgusted by her. He only wanted to get out of her influence, out of the reach of her eyes and her voice, steel-sharp the one, mad-hard the other, except when it wheedled and coaxed. He had undertaken this third task. It mattered nothing to him. It would soon be done, and he could be on his way to the outlaws, to death, to whatever might be the end of his long march.

The woman had brought with her, slung on her back, a wide basket of woven withies. She set it down at the well's edge, took from inside it a coil of rope, one end fastened to the handle of the basket. The soldier looked at it with a dull interest. It seemed sound and well made. The woman passed the rope over the wheel, looped it twice round the alder trunk, dropped the basket over the well's edge till it hung just below the level of the ground.

'Step into the basket.'

'Why not you? Then you may get your own light. I have strength to let you down and haul you up. I am stronger than you.'

'Not so. I can handle a rope, soldier. I have been to sea.'

The man shrugged his shoulders. What did it matter? Against so set a will he had not the strength of mind to resist.

Steadying himself by pulling with one hand on the rope that suspended the basket from the wheel, he stepped into the well-mouth. The rope held, the basket creaked and strained as it took his weight. In truth it would have held more than his lean and wasted body. The basket was a yard deep or thereabouts, and wide enough to have held two. The soldier had not taken his knapsack from his shoulders. He desired to be ready to go as soon as his task was done. Taut round the alder trunk, the rope stretched and strained, but did not give. Slowly the woman let it pass round the trunk, and smoothly the soldier descended into the well. He looked up. The woman, some paces back from the well, was no longer visible, and all the soldier could see was the ferns and nettles that fringed the top of the well, the wheel on its axle, the slowly diminishing circle of the blue morning sky, broken by the gently moving tree branches. The wheel, unused and unoiled, complained like a crone in a winter wind, pitying herself. The well was deep – how deep he could not tell. Down he went, till the sky was no bigger than the bottom of a bucket, and the whimpering wheel was heard no more. The woman must be strong, so smoothly did she lower the basket, letting the rope slide steadily round the alder trunk.

Now when all daylight had gone, the basket touched bottom, and the light from the blue flame was the only light to be seen. The soldier held his breath, but not from fear. To reach the flame, he had to lift one leg out of the basket, hold on to the rope with one hand, stretch to the floor with the other. His hand approached the thing with caution. But it had no heat in it. He held in his hand what seemed to be a small earthenware jar whose colour he could not see and whose shape he could feel as round and bulging, yet quite small, no bigger than a hen's egg. From its top issued a bluish flame, clear and not smoky, burning steadily except when his hand shook, and then it flickered and wavered, now and again becoming completely extinguished, until the steadying of the hand restored its original constancy. Cautiously the soldier blew on it: the flame disappeared, but burned again when his breath was withdrawn. Then the rope tightened, and very slowly the basket was raised. As daylight once more made the well-sides visible, and the complaints of the wheel became audible, it was like the ending of a dream. Not steadily, as in the descent, but more jerkily, more slowly, the basket was drawn up. At length the soldier's head was within a few inches of ground level. After another pull by the woman he would be able to put his free hand on the well-mouth and heave himself out.

But the woman pulled no more. She grasped the rope firmly and, keeping it coiled twice about the alder trunk, approached the well's edge till the soldier could see her fully.

'The light!' she said. 'Hand up the light.'

Looking into the woman's steel-hard, glittering eyes, the soldier was suddenly aware, blindingly aware, of an expression of concentrated cunning and malevolence such as he had never seen before. In the voice he heard triumph, but only the evil in her face betrayed her intention, betrayed it beyond the power of even the blindest of men not to discern. He tried not to show his apprehension, said steadily in cool, almost casual tones:

'I will give you the light the instant that both my feet are set upon firm ground.'

'Hand me the light, I say, before you drop it.'

'As soon as you draw me from the well and I am on firm ground.'

'No! no, pretty soldier, I must have it now.'

Clasping the rope tightly in her left hand, she stepped quickly to the very edge of the well, leaned down and snatched at the flame with her right hand. The soldier, though he had foreseen her coming, had not allowed for her swiftness.

He tried to clasp the well's edge with his maimed left hand, missed it, and made a grab for the axle above his head. It was beyond his reach. But in making the effort, he jerked the flame free from the woman's grasp, lost his hold of it and saw it hit the top of the basket and roll over the edge into the well. The flame disappeared, and he heard the pot echo as it hit the side of the well, and then the bottom.

The woman shrieked a curse more fierce and inhuman than the soldier had ever heard in his life. It was as if a fiend was screaming in hell. Already she had loosened her hold on the rope, and the basket began to drop.

'You may keep the flame! You may keep it till your eyes rot in your head. You may spend eternity with it, and may the devil take your soul as his worms will have your living body!'

The woman's words became incoherent. The soldier was aware only of her screams of fury and malice. In terror he tried to grasp at the sides of the well, but he was dropping too fast. In any event the well's sides were too smooth, too slimed with rotted growths and decaying fungus, to allow of any hold. The soldier groaned as the basket's pace slackened. Evidently he was not to be hurled to a sudden death, shattered on the floor of the well. Instead, he was lowered with decreasing speed. Very faintly he heard the witch's imprecations, saw once more the daylight dwindle and die.

He was powerless. Once, indeed, he raised his voice in a great shout for mercy, but the woman paid no heed, and the pace of the descent did not alter. At the bottom of the shaft there was silence. Bruised but not much hurt, numb with ultimate despair, the soldier waited. He felt the rope, to which he still clung, grow slack. Then suddenly it fell upon him in a tangled mass. The woman had unlooped it from the tree and flung it after the man. He had no longer any possible means of escape. The end.

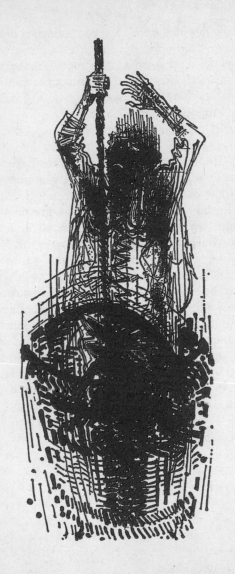

C.F.—3

This could not be the end. The end was never meant to be like this.

'Get me out! Send down another rope. Woman, woman, I say! Get me out! How long do you mean to keep me here. Get me out, and I will do whatever you wish. I will be your slave, your lover. Get me out, I say!'

Exhausted with shouting, the soldier dropped down into the basket. She could not have heard him, even if she had wanted to. He was entirely at her mercy. He dared not allow himself the hope that she would have pity on him. How can any man know what he hopes? Did he wish to live? He knew only that he did not wish to die like that, gradually fainting from hunger, perhaps first losing his reason. He had been a soldier. He would gladly have died fighting. But to die of mere exhaustion, to be extinguished slowly – this was too horrible to think of. Yet think of it he must. How greatly must his body suffer before the final sleep? He had known hunger before, many a time, on the march. He had felt hunger till his belly cried out and his whole body fainted. How much further could his body endure before its final extinction? It was no matter. He had nothing to live for, except to put off death. Even vengeance for the outrage that had sent him out into the world with one silver dollar seemed to him of no importance.

7. *The Tobacco-pipe*

He must have swooned from terror and exhaustion, for he was next aware of waking – after how long he did not know: it might have been minutes, hours, days. When he awoke, he was conscious only of a dim radiance that came from the blue flame, still burning on the floor of the well. His mind was composed. There was nothing to be done, nothing to fear, nothing to hope except that his end might be calm and without pain. He put aside the thought of taking his own life. He had no knife, and there was nothing from which to suspend the rope. The blue flame showed him vaguely the sides and bottom of the well. All was dark, streaked with slime and decay. There was no handhold or foothold by which he could raise himself even a few feet from the bottom. Evidently no creature beside himself was alive in that unearthy place.

More accustomed now to the faint and feeble light, his eyes could make out a few scattered bones – human bones and a skull, small and cracked, lying against one wall of the well-shaft. A gentle, scarcely conscious wave of pity passed through him. He desired not to think, he must do anything to keep from thinking. He remembered his flute, the companion of his marching, the means by which he had whiled away empty hours in camp or at a tavern. Sitting now on the basket, out of which he had rolled while he was unconscious, he loosened the straps of his knapsack and fumbled inside it. He took out the flute and put it to his lips, paused for a moment to recollect a tune, then played the first notes of a camp song. The tune was plaintive, and in the darkness and hollowness of his prison unbearable. He pushed the instru-

ment back into his knapsack, overwhelmed by a great wave
of despair, against which he fought desperately. Yet he half-
wished it would annihilate him, so that he could swoon once
more and perhaps remain unconscious for ever. His hand,
pushing the flute into the bag, stumbled on something which
made him pause. At first he could not identify it. Then suddenly he recognised an object whose existence he had quite
forgotten – a pipe of another sort, a clay tobacco-pipe. With

this he had often solaced himself of an evening, but lately he had forgotten its existence, for he had no money with which to buy tobacco. He found that the bowl of the pipe was half full. Evidently it had gone out the last time he had smoked it and, lacking a light, he had never finished it. How dearly he would have enjoyed a last pipe of tobacco. This was not withheld even from men condemned to death by hanging or by gunfire. He had no tinderbox, no means of drawing the soothing vapour into his mouth and lungs. But what of the flame in the little jar? He had scarcely given it a thought, but now he reached out and picked it up. He had noticed before that it was without heat. But there was no harm in making the experiment. He held the flame to the pipe-bowl and began to suck in.

Nothing mattered but that the tobacco should ignite. The soldier feared that it had become damp, or that the flame would have no power, and he would be cheated of his last comfort. His last comfort on earth. Was he truly on earth – or rather, was he not beneath it? The flame died as he drew it into the clay bowl of the pipe, brightened as he released it to take breath. Presently, with indescribable satisfaction, he became conscious of the sweet taste of tobacco smoke on his tongue. He pulled deeply on the pipe, filled his mouth with smoke, and then released it into the obscurity around him.

In the midst of the smoke cloud something glowed with a dusky light, dimmer and deeper in tone than the blue flame

which now shone as before in the little stoneware jar, grasped still in the soldier's right hand. The something in the smoke cloud was in the shape of a man, but no greater than four or five inches in height. As the smoke cleared, the soldier saw that a manikin was indeed standing before him, as he sat on the overturned basket. It was almost black and quite naked, illuminated faintly by the dusky radiance which came from itself. It resembled some demon or imp he had once seen engraved in a book; it was in a priest's house where he had been billeted. The demon grinned and smirked from under its shaggy hair. The soldier could not discern if it was in all parts exactly like a man, for its loins were thickly overgrown with fine black hair. The demon bowed long before the soldier and stood waiting.

He felt a sense of wonder, but no fear. How could a soldier, or any man for the matter of that, fear a creature so diminutive, unarmed and naked? The soldier took another puff at his tobacco-pipe, and as the demon said nothing but continued to bow before him as if awaiting orders, at last he spoke.

'What are you? Why are you here? Have you come to mock at me in my last hours, appearing to me in the likeness of a devil?'

The manikin stopped grinning and bowing, appearing to be offended by this question.

'I am at your command. As master of the flame, you have it in your power to summon me, and I cannot refuse.'

The voice was small but clear, light in tone, smooth, and of a gentlemanly way of speech.

'Are you angel or devil? Are you from Heaven or Hell?'

'Evil is as evil does,' responded the demon glibly, 'good as good.'

'You had better get out of here if you can. As I am to die, I'll not spend my last hours in the company of a spirit.'

'I am your servant, but you cannot dismiss me. It might be that I could help you.'

The demon looked infinitely cunning, and at the same time innocent, like a child caught stealing some trifle.

The soldier, though he did not doubt the reality of the demon – he had been brought up to credit the existence of such creatures, had spoken to many who claimed to have seen them – had no belief in the creature's power to perform any effective action, much less to be of help to him.

He laughed grimly and said, half in jest :

'If you have power to do as I wish, then destroy that vile woman who sent me down into this hole.'

The demon bowed, smiled as if in satisfaction at having received an order.

'It shall be done, master. What more?'

'Get me out of here. If you can do that, I shall be the first to own that you have powers beyond your size.'

For answer the demon grinned once more and skipped to the other side of the well, behind the basket, which lay where it had rolled when the soldier tumbled out of it. He beckoned to the soldier to follow him. The soldier, puffing on the last of his tobacco, got stiffly to his feet, shouldered his knapsack, kept tight hold of the jar containing the blue flame. By its light he saw that the demon was perched on a stone jutting out a mere inch from the well, some two feet above the well floor. He grasped a rusted iron ring protruding from the wall beside him. The demon let go of the ring and jumped on to his master's shoulder, putting his lips to the man's ear. The soldier had no time to be surprised at the demon's preter-natural power of levitation; scarcely knowing what he was doing, yet certain that he must do it, he tugged at the ring, expecting it to come away in his hands or crumble into rust-eaten fragments. He was not prepared to see a narrow but tall opening appear in the wall in front of him. Yet when it so appeared, it seemed the most natural thing in the world – in the half-world, that is, of evil, despair and mystery into which he had been dropped. He paused, trying to see into the darkness beyond the hole in the well's side.

'Come, let us be gone,' the demon said with some urgency into the soldier's ear.

The soldier stepped into the opening and began to grope his way forward.

8. The Escape

In the passage it was light enough for the soldier to make his way, stooping and stumbling towards whatever end it led to. In his knapsack he had nothing but his flute and the little jar containing the blue flame. His cudgel he had lost long before. The light in the stone passage was dim, coming from what source he could not tell. With him went his diminutive companion, the smoky black demon, now perched on his shoulder, now floating on ahead, turning occasionally to grin or beckon. The passage led gradually upwards. About his direction the soldier could tell nothing. To his dazed mind and bruised body it meant something he had not known for many days – hope. Hope of what? He did not know. Hope of life, perhaps, hope of not dying like a forgotten prisoner in a dungeon. The problem of what use his life was to him hardly presented itself. As a soldier he had been used to action – to inaction also, to be sure, but not the inaction of doing nothing because he could not move. Here at last he could move, hard though the going was.

The demon darted on before him, then stopped, gesturing. 'Take what you want. You will need all you can carry.'

The soldier stopped and looked about him, puzzled. He had hardly noticed his immediate surroundings, so intent had he been on putting as much ground as possible between him and his loathsome prison. The walls of the passage were of stone, like those of the well. As the ground gained height, the clamminess of the walls gradually gave way to a drier surface, and the fungus was replaced by lichen and little trailing plants, miniature ivy and ferns. But it was evidently not these that the demon indicated. Here and there, at irregular intervals along the passage, were shallow recesses or ledges in the stone-work, and these, the soldier now perceived, held a variety of objects. There were plates, goblets, trinkets of one kind and another, all rusted, tarnished, covered with mould or moss.

'These are her treasures – things she has wheedled or stolen. Fill your bag. You will need them.'

The soldier did as he was bidden. He had no knowledge of such ware, but he picked up here a dish, there a cup, hesitated until the demon nodded approval, and stowed it in his knap-sack. The dull clink of object on object confirmed his impression that they were of metal, though whether precious or not he could not tell. The heavier and duller objects he took to be pewter, and left them where they were. There were other things of no value – bottles, leather cases green with mould, a holster with no pistol in it, a powder flask, an ink-horn, a leather belt, rolls of parchment, a boot, a tinder-box, a skein of hair, a skull. The soldier passed over these things with in-difference or disgust. He took only what seemed to be of value, what seemed his due. He found a string of beads, dully gleam-ing, a bag of coins, a gold brooch, a buckle, rings set with stones.

So absorbed was the soldier in the business of looting that he scarcely noticed the appearance of unmistakable daylight, filtering greenly through the obscurity before him. Nor had he become aware of something else. The tobacco-pipe which he had lit from the blue flame was still between his teeth, but it had gone out. His pipe had been only half full, and now the tobacco was all consumed. The soldier knocked out the dottle and put the pipe in his pocket.

'Master, I must leave you. Be careful, your treasure will breed danger, though it will be of use. If you have need of a horse, you have means to get one. When you need me, you have but to light your pipe at the flame. I will come.'

The soldier desired to know where he was, to seek advice as to what he should do next, to offer the demon thanks for his services. But when he looked in the direction of the little sharp voice, the demon was not to be seen.

As if in a dream, the soldier lifted his knapsack, now heavy with metal, higher on his back, and climbed a flight of rough steps down which streamed green daylight, almost dazzling after the obscurity of the passage. He was in the open air, under the trees. The sky was dull, threatening rain. He had no idea what time of day it was, but he guessed it was late afternoon. He had nothing with which to cut himself a staff or cudgel, so he broke a slender branch from a tree and trimmed it as best he could. There was no sign of the witch or of her evil dwelling. All thought of finding her and exacting punishment was driven from his mind by the thought of freedom and the loathing he felt for her and all her ways. The trees were not thick, but there was no sign of track or pathway. Suddenly a rabbit broke from the undergrowth behind him and made off to his right. The soldier went to the left. It seemed as good a way as any. Perhaps he was influenced by a subconscious suspicion that the creature was one of the witch's familiars and would lead him back to her or to some other danger.

The woods thinned to a sort of common or heathland, on which grew infrequent, stunted oaks, gorse bushes and patches of scrub and nettle. The birds sang, muted in the dull evening light. No other creature was to be heard or seen. There was nothing to do but to trudge on. Hunger was added to fatigue, but hope, newborn though undefined, for the time being surpassed both. He was used to trudging. The way could not go on for ever.

9. 'The Wanton Child'

Across the moor, under the grey sky, came a sound, a sound of hooves. As the soldier directed his steps to where the sound came from, he muttered to himself :

'A horse. It is mine, one way or another.'

His unshaven chin was set grimly, his stick grasped with resolution. To the sound of hooves, slow and measured, muffled by the heathy soil – for there was evidently no road – was added another sound, that of a man singing. The voice came in broken snatches, as though the singer – if such he could be called – was half-asleep.

Rounding a thicket of thorn bushes, the soldier saw the figure of a man sitting awkwardly astride a grey horse whose reins dangled limply over the animal's neck. The man's voice rose in an effort to reach the higher notes of some campaigning song whose words he had evidently forgotten. The tune failed and was succeeded by an oath as the horse stumbled on a tussock of grass. The rider, whom the soldier now made out to be an army captain far gone in drink, lolled sideways. As the soldier ran forward instinctively, to prevent a fall, the captain slipped sideways, rolled out of the saddle and came to rest on the ground, one foot still in its stirrup.

The horse whinnied; the soldier grasped the rein in one hand and, throwing aside his cudgel, tried to free the captain's foot from the stirrup with the other.

'I need your horse,' said the soldier. 'You'll be better without it.'

'I care not. Take the cursed bitch and . . .'

He hiccuped, groaned, subsided on to his back as the soldier got his leg free.

'You have come from the city?'

The captain said nothing. Drink had made him almost unconscious. The soldier looked down at him with involuntary disgust. The grey horse stood passive beside him. He loosened the captain's sword-belt, from which hung a sword in its scabbard, and fastened it round his own waist.

'I need this too, captain. I will pay for it.'

He took from his knapsack two coins, of whose value he was not sure, and thrust them into the drunk man's pocket.

'It will rain before tonight,' he said disdainfully. 'That should sober you. Lie easy. The grass is soft. May the god of battle protect you till cockcrow.'

Then he turned to the horse, made fast the saddle girths, put his foot in the stirrup, mounted. Stiff as always from his wounds, and cumbered with the captain's sword, he mounted clumsily, but he had ridden before, and the horse responded readily to his tongue and hand.

'Get moving, my beauty. Take me back where you came from.'

If there was drink, there was an inn. That was all he needed. He wheeled the horse about and urged it at a brisk pace along the path by which it had come. Before long he struck the highroad and, freshened by the wind upon which he could sense the first drops of rain, he gave the horse its head. For the best part of an hour he rode at a steady trot, without any sign of habitation or of any other mortal being. The sky grew darker. At length, breasting a hill, he made out in the twilight the roofs of the city and a few lighted windows. Good. He would find shelter from the rain, rest for the night. Before long the well-known streets resounded to his horse's hooves as they clattered on the cobbles. At a walking pace the horse carried the soldier up the high street to the market square. All

at once the soldier felt imperatively the need for food, drink, rest.

In the yard of 'The Wanton Child', the principal inn in that quarter of the city, he dismounted and gave the reins to a stableboy.

'Take this beast to the barracks. It belongs there.'

The boy hesitated, scratching his head in perplexity. The soldier spoke quietly, authoritatively, but the order was unusual. The landlord came forward from a doorway.

'If you are the landlord, tell the boy to do as I say.'

The soldier's hand was on the pommel of his sword.

'Do as the gentleman says.'

As the boy led the horse away, the soldier turned to the landlord.

'A room, landlord – the best you have. Hot water. Then food and wine.'

'Also the best?'

The landlord spoke with irony, gazing contemptuously at the soldier's ragged clothing, unkempt appearance.

'I have ridden far. I can pay.'

The landlord nodded submissively.

'Then send for a barber, and a man who deals in gold and silver ware. In the morning send a tailor and a bootmaker. See this is done.'

'It is late. The gentleman had better wait till tomorrow.'

'Then send for a barber at least. A man cannot dine at ease with a chin like mine.'

The landlord nodded once more and signed to the soldier to follow him in. He was submissive but not subservient.

'Perhaps I should buy a little more civility. Here. This should add sauce to the meal you are about to prepare, speed to the barber's legs, and a certain sweetness to your tongue.'

He pushed a handful of silver coins into the landlord's grasp. The landlord, taken aback but considerably mollified, threw open the door of a big, comfortable room on the first floor.

'It will do. When I am shaved and washed, you may send up the cook.'

'With pleasure. Your honour will perhaps allow me to select the wine myself.'

The soldier nodded.

The landlord, about to withdraw, stood for a moment in the doorway.

'The tailor and the other gentleman you wish to see – a goldsmith, was it? – your honour had better send for in the morning. They should be ready to wait on you after the hanging.'

'The hanging?'

The landlord motioned the soldier to step across the landing and look through the open door of a room in the front of the house.

'I beg your pardon. It is too dark to see. This afternoon a gallows was set up yonder. Tomorrow, early, they are hanging a witch. All the town will be out to see.'

The soldier shuddered grimly.

'I have seen enough hangings in my time.'

'The troopers took her today. The judges had long wanted her for evil practices. Justice was swift. They said she had caused the deaths of many.'

The soldier said nothing, feeling neither triumph nor remorse. He had no doubt that the condemned woman was she under whose roof he had sheltered. He returned to his room, calling to the landlord, as if in consequence of his train of thought.

'Tobacco, landlord. Send up tobacco – the best you can get.'

10. The Command

Washed and barbered, the soldier felt better. His spirits improved, and when his meal was brought, he was hungry enough to have done with humbler fare than 'The Wanton Child' was accustomed to provide. The table was celebrated. The wine too was excellent. Eating and drinking slowly and with relish, he felt at ease as he listened to the gentle but constant sound of the rain falling outside, the laughter and ribaldry from the taproom beneath. The sounds came muffled and indistinct, mingled with the twanging of a stringed instrument, a snatch of song, a murmur of applause. The soldier would at another time have gone down and joined the company, but now he was in the mood to be alone and savour his new freedom. Only his old and tattered clothes irked him. Tomorrow would remedy that. In the meantime he was content enough to muse on his altered fortune, to stretch his sore limbs, to think of nothing but the well-being of the moment.

The room in which he sat, enjoying his food and wine, was handsome in a faded way, overfurnished but comfortable. In a smaller room or alcove, curtained off, was the bed. The soldier had tested it and found it soft enough. For the present, however, he had no mind to sleep. For a long time he sat, until sounds of the scraping of boots, of pots set down empty, of fuddled goodnights, betokened the breaking up of the company beneath. Then he rose and went to the door, calling down for a servant to come and attend to him.

'If the singer has not gone, send him up. You may leave the dishes till morning, but I will have more wine.'

The blind singer stumbled up the stairs with a cithern in one hand, a stick in the other. He was old and poor, his clothes rusty, frayed at the folds, soiled with age and neglect. The servant led him to a stool in a corner of the room, and withdrew, closing the door behind him.

With quavering voice and hesitant fingers plucking the strings of his instrument, the man made tolerable music. He sang of war, of love, of drinking, of youth and age. The soldier filled and refilled his own glass, put a can of wine into the old man's hand to refresh him. The man drank, answered the soldier's questions about his life and fortunes. The man spoke hesitatingly, fumbling for words, patching together a story of misfortune, blindness from youth, near-starvation, comparative security in old age, now that he was sought for to entertain humble company in the city.

The soldier listened, seemingly unmoved yet taking in his story with grave attention. Then at length he took the old man's empty can from his fingers, placed the cithern once more in his grasp.

'It is late. Tune up, old man, and let us have one last song.'

The musician obeyed, adjusting the strings till they were well enough in tune.

'A love song, sir? The song of Phyllis and her Corydon? A song of Diana and the hunting?'

'No.'

'A song of parting then?'

'Not that.'

'A country song perhaps. A merry tale of the lawyer that was cheated by a milkmaid.'

'What you will, musician, but not that.'

'Then, sir, you shall have a song of tobacco – a song neither of love nor of the gods nor of merriment, but a good song of the weed.'

Without further speech the old man cleared his throat,

played a brief prelude and began searching his mind for the words and filling the gaps by plucking at his instrument. The effect was one of pathos, and not that intended by the unknown composer.

> 'Come, Sirrah Jack O,
> Bring some tobacco.
> Haste away,
> Quick, I say,

Do not stay,
Shun delay,
For I drank none good today.
I swear this tobacco
Is perfect Trinidado.
By the mass
Never was
Better gear
Than is here;
By the rood,
For the blood,
It is very good.
For those that do condemn it
And such as not commend it,
Let them go
Pluck a crow
And not know
As I do,
The sweet of Trinidado.'

'You have reminded me, old fellow, of what I had almost forgotten. Will you take a pipe before you go?'

'Of what use is tobacco to a blind singer? I thank you, but it is no pleasure to me unless I can see the smoke rising, and in truth it does my voice no good. If you have finished, sir, I will go to my bed.'

'As you wish. Here is money for you, and let me help you down the stairs.'

He gave the old man money, helped him to his feet, saw him safely to the head of the stair and heard him tap his way out of earshot. Then he shut the door, returned to his chair at the table, poured out the end of the wine.

'A malediction,' he said to himself, raising his glass, sudden bitterness in his tone. 'Ill health to the King, to his justices, and all that drive poor ballad-singers and soldiers from their doors!'

He drained the glass, set it down, fumbled for his pipe at the bottom of his knapsack. This he filled with tobacco from what the landlord had brought him, and felt in his knapsack once again, this time for the little jar in which the blue flame still flickered and glowed.

'Come, devil or whatever you are!' the soldier said, drawing the flame into the bowl of the pipe. 'Were you a dream or are you indeed at my command, as once you said?'

'No devil, master, but at your command. What is your desire?'

The near-black manikin stood on the table before the soldier, grinning and bowing.

'This room – look at it. It is dirty. It needs sweeping. I do not care for disorder. I am – or I was – a soldier, and I care not to see my quarters at sixes and sevens.'

'It shall be cleaned, master. Nothing easier.'

The demon spoke rapidly, eagerly, and skipped towards a cupboard in one corner of the room.

'Come back, do you hear! It is not you who shall clean out my quarters. I will have a servant fit for a gentleman.'

'As you wish. Whom shall I summon?'

The demon stood once more on the table. The soldier thumped upon it and spoke threateningly, as one determined to be obeyed.

'Fetch me the King's daughter! None but she shall be my chambermaid. Do you hear?'

'I can do it, your honour. But it is dangerous.'

'Do as I say.'

Still the demon hesitated, motionless upon the table.

'Fetch me the Princess – if you can.'

'I can do it, master. I have great power, and I must do it if you desire. I am your servant, so long as you possess the flame. Summon me, and I am bound to obey, but it is also my duty to protect you. It is a servant's duty to protect his master. What you command is perilous. The King is strong. It will be death to one who mishandles the Princess.'

The demon spoke with growing urgency, half-pleading, half-threatening. The soldier was unmoved.

'Do as I command, if you are here to be commanded.'

The demon shrugged his black, lean shoulders.

'So be it, but I have warned you.'

In a dark swirl, almost silently, the demon was gone. The soldier had risen from his chair. Now he strode this way and that about the disordered room, pausing to puff agitatedly at the tobacco-pipe. He went to the window, opened the shutters, gazed out at the silent town. The rain had stopped. Only a few scattered lights showed that here and there someone was awake. A dog howled in the distance. With a shiver the soldier closed the shutters, returned to his seat. Calmer now, he pulled steadily at the pipe until, as he drew smoke from the final crumbs of tobacco at the bottom of the bowl, the sound of midnight began to fall from a distant steeple.

11. *The Princess*

Sunlight came over the wooded hills to the east of the city, caught the weathercock on the topmost tower of the castle, crept slowly downward into the Princess's chamber. The Princess did not stir, though the pigeons in the gutters trilled as loudly as ever, and the bells in all the steeples insisted clamorously upon each of the quarters. In the yard the sentries went off duty, yawning, and were relieved by others. Horses in the stables stamped and pawed. Maids and grooms were astir, but the Princess's maid could not wake her mistress.

'Let her sleep,' said the King's steward. 'The dressmakers can wait. She needs her sleep now. I guess the Count will keep her waking, once she is a bride.'

The morning wore on. Clerks and stallkeepers hurried here and there in the streets; carters cursed; dogs fouled the walls; the tongues of rumour wagged. The dressmakers frowned and tapped their feet in the ante-room, gossiping. Spite and intrigue ranged the corridors. It had been an uneasy place, the castle, since the Queen's death. The King, who had not remarried, brooded, ran his affairs with cold efficiency, caring only for his daughter, all that his Queen had left.

'Let her sleep. She has no need to be stirring.'

'Her breakfast is cold. The dressmakers have gone away.'

'They can come back tomorrow – and the next day if need be – and the next.'

'The Count will not wait for ever, sire. She has put him off twice already.'

But the Princess came at last into the King's room, her night-clothes covered by a blue robe edged with gold, her fair hair, undressed, falling behind her bowed shoulders. She looked as if she were bearing an unseen load. Her pale face, paler than usual, seemed to be that of one in a dream. Her eyes had the dark-circled brightness of one wakened too soon from sleep. She sank on to a stool at her father's feet, resting her hands on his knees, her chin on her hands.

'Leave us.'

For minutes the Princess said nothing.

'No breakfast?'

She shook her head.

'No sleep?'

'I slept late. I had a dream. I think it was a dream.'

She stared straight into her father's eyes. He frowned a little, noting a dull, flushed patch on her left cheek. The Count would wish her to look her best.

'Tell me.'

'I hardly know where it began. I don't know how long I had been sleeping before I started to dream. The clocks were striking as I got out of bed and was drawn from my room, along the corridors, downstairs, through the dark rooms and out into the yard. I don't know how many hours were struck. None of the dogs barked, no sentry stirred; I saw my way, though the night was dark.'

'What made you rise?'

'An unseen hand. It took mine and pulled me on. I could not resist. I was not cold, though I had only my night-clothes on. We went down the hill, over the cobbles, through the dark streets. We turned corners, crossed the square. At last we entered a house. Upstairs I went into a room I had never seen before. In it was a man. He sat beside a table. There were dishes beside him, and an empty glass. I think he had been smoking, for even now I can remember the smell of tobacco. It was very vivid, very clear.'

'How came you by that mark on your left cheek?'

The Princess put her hand to her face.

'That must be where his boot hit me.'

'His boot? What are you saying? You tell me this was a dream?'

'How should I know? Do you know always the difference between truth and a dream, father?'

'I never dream. So the man threw his boot at you? What sort of man was this?'

'A rough man.'

'It would seem so. But go on.'

'He said, if I remember right, "So you have come – Your Highness".'

'He called you "Your Highness"?'

'But it seemed as if he was mocking me a little. I said he was rough: I mean, he *looked* rough. Yet he spoke not roughly. His clothes were poor. When he told me to clear up the dishes and sweep the floor, he sounded not unkind.'

'Sweep the floor? He made you sweep the floor?'

'There were brooms and brushes in a cupboard. I obeyed. I had no strength to do otherwise.'

'He forced you?'

The King's indignation grew, his brow became darker, his face more flushed. Yet it was only a dream. . . . But the mark on his daughter's face . . .

'No. He scarcely moved, but sat still watching me. I remember his eyes. They were deep sunk and seemed to. . . . I hardly know how to say it : they seemed to hold me under his will. Yet I felt no resentment. He looked sad and bitter. I found I did not mind doing his bidding.'

'Indeed ! Is this a fit confession for my daughter?'

'I say only what happened. It was a dream. There was weariness in his voice, as well as sadness. I have sometimes felt sad and weary. You know how it is, father.'

'If I feel sad, I call for wine and my fool. If weary, I go to sleep. But go on. What was this man like? Was it someone you knew?'

'I had the feeling I had seen his face before, but I don't know where or when, or who it was. In dreams it is often so. As I swept the floor I seemed unable to resist his wishes, and unwilling. He spoke little, only telling me not to miss anything, but to sweep his room as clean as our rooms are swept in the castle. When I had made all straight, he yawned and said he would go to bed. He told me to help him off with his boots. He was stiff, he said, and his limbs ached. They were rough boots, worn and heavy, but not dirty. I knelt and pulled.'

'You knelt before this man, this ruffian?'

'There was no other way. I pulled at one, he tried to loosen the other. At last mine came off. I staggered back against the wall. It was then that he got the other boot off and threw it at me. The effort of getting them off, and my slowness – for the boots were on very tight, and I had never done this before – had made him suddenly angry. The boot he threw did not hurt me. "Now clean them," he said. I got a cloth from the cupboard and rubbed and scoured till the boots were as bright as I could make them. As I rubbed and polished, he took up a flute that he had and began to blow into it, fixing his eyes on me all the time. Then he threw down the flute, for the notes would not come right. His fingers fumbled, and the sound he made was windy and not true. "Would you like to hear me play?" he asked me. But I said nothing. Then as I finished polishing the boots and stood them in a corner, I heard the first cock, far away beyond the city. I told him I had to go. I don't know why I said this, but it seemed to me like a summons to return home. The man said nothing, but rose and opened the door for me. As he did so, I seemed to feel again the unseen hand clasping mine and leading me out of the room. When I crossed the threshold, it was as if his eyes were boring into my back. But I did not turn. I don't recall the journey home, nor how I got here, nor how soon I fell asleep. When I awoke this morning, I was very tired. My back and arms still ache. But I feel no pain.'

The King said nothing, his brow still cleft with a deep frown, his cheeks flushed with anger.

'I almost forgot: I think the man's last words to me were, "Goodnight, Your Highness. You shall come again" – or something like that. I forget his actual words. But his voice was not unkind, and he seemed no longer angry at my clumsiness with the boots.'

'Where was this house you speak of? What was it like? What sort of room were you in? Which way did you go, and how long did the journey take?'

But the Princess could remember little of this, and at last she said she would go and sit for a while in the garden.

'Think no more of my dream, father,' she said, kissing him and smoothing back his hair.

But the King thought of it much, and later spoke of it to his steward.

'I tell you, it was no dream. It is witchcraft – witchcraft and false practice. I fear for the Princess.'

'It is better not to fear, sire,' the steward said with that air of wisdom he had found it prudent to adopt when desiring neither to gainsay nor to support his master.

'It is witchcraft. What was it you told me that woman said this morning on the gallows?'

'The evil woman who was hung at Your Majesty's command –'

'It was not at my command. It was on the verdict of the judges. Be careful what you say.'

'– on the command of Your Majesty's judges: this woman is said to have died cursing Your Majesty. I know not what she said, for I was not there. It is all hearsay. Such words from such a woman were to be expected. I beg Your Majesty to have no fear from the words of such a creature.'

'Why was she put to death?'

'She carried on false practices against the laws of God and man. She brought about the destruction of more than one man in the city.'

'Ah! so you grant she has evil powers.'

'This is what the witnesses *said*, sire.'

The man's tones were as glossy as the velvet of his tunic.

'For all I know, the woman's victims well deserved their lot. Nevertheless, they pined away unaccountably, and the doctors were baffled. To receive such a woman's curse is not comfortable, even for a man of sense.'

'A man of sense, sire, *and* of good conscience.'

The flattery was manifest, and expected. It was part of the duties of the steward.

'Nevertheless, if the woman had evil power, and if she has left evil agents and familiars, they must be hunted out and destroyed. If necessary, we must use force – scour the city, the whole kingdom if need be.'

'Such a spiriting hence, sire, as Her Highness describes can hardly be countered by force. In such an affair, the better counsel would be to use craft. We must make preparations for a repetition of this dream. If, as I forecast, nothing more takes place to endanger the Princess, there is no harm done. But it is well to be prepared. The first thing, as I see it, is to find if this house, this room, exists in the city, for we can do nothing without that knowledge. But craft, I think, is to be used in such dealings. I know a man skilled in sorcery . . .'

12. *The Danger*

'Perhaps the company would favour a ballad with a chorus,' the blind musician said, 'a song they could join in.'

The company in the soldier's room at 'The Wanton Child' assented, the musician passed his fingers across the strings of his cithern, began in a mournful enough voice:

> 'Young Johnny was a soldier in the devil's own war –'

The soldier joined in:

> 'Then pass up the bottle and never run dry.'

The musician continued:

> 'He was wounded in the right leg, in the right leg so
>   sore,
> And sorrow's the ocean will never run dry.

In his fine new clothes the soldier was not well at ease, but the singing and the wine were beginning to induce a relaxed mood.

> 'Young Johnny he was wounded in the right leg so
>   sore,
> Then pass up the bottle and never run dry.
> When his leg was mended, he went marching once
>   more,
> And sorrow's the ocean will never run dry.'

The regimental drummer, an old comrade, hauled the wench on to his knees as he sat at the table, and both joined in the lines of the refrain. It was a good song, though the melody was over-melancholy for the mood of the company.

Returning from his visits to the clothier and the man to
whom he had sold most of his gold and silver ware, the soldier
had fallen in with his old comrade-in-arms and bidden him to
supper. The drummer, a good fellow though of commoner
make than the soldier, had arrived in company with a young
woman to entertain him for the evening. She was bold and
coarse, a frequent companion to the drummer, well used to his
endearments. The soldier had not greatly liked the company,
but he felt the need for society, and when his two guests had
tired of chaffing him over his new-gotten finery, they settled
down to enjoy his hospitality.

'You have found a fairy godmother, soldier, I don't doubt.'

'A godmother, you may say, but no fairy. Drink up, and
ask not where the wine comes from.'

> 'He was wounded for a second time in his right arm,
> Then pass up the bottle and never run dry.
> Young Johnny went home and was cured of his
>   harm,
> And sorrow's the ocean will never run dry.

> 'Young Johnny was wounded, he was wounded in the
>   heart,
> Then pass up the bottle and never run dry.
> But he could find no surgeon to heal him of his
>   smart,
> And sorrow's the ocean will never run dry.

> 'Young Johnny for to cure him of this grievous sore,
> Then pass up the bottle and never run dry,
> Went marching right back again to the devil's own
>   war,
> And sorrow's the ocean will never run dry.'

'Your wine is good, friend. Your meat is good. It is a pity
you have no sweetheart.'

'The venison, I fancy, was poached from the King. It

tastes the sweeter for that. The landlord gave me a hint of it, but you had best say nothing. He keeps a good table, and the fewer questions are asked the better.'

'He has sweeter meat for the poaching than any venison that runs in his forest. The Count will be a happy man when he takes his Princess to wife. Now there's meat would be worth the stealing.'

'Peace, drummer. I warrant there's more meat on your lap

at this hour than any scrag-end of a princess. Pay heed to what's your own, old man.'

The wench tightened her hold on the drummer, wove her ringed fingers into his hair. Then she took the cup from his hand and drained it herself, paying her man for his loss with a bibulous kiss. Both laughed.

The soldier, in no mood to join in, left them to each other's entertainment, bade the minstrel sing another song. He complied, the soldier paid him off, saw him down the stairs. Returning, he found his guests had retired into the half-dark of the alcove. He poured more wine, drank deep, took out his tobacco-pipe and filled it. He changed his mind, left it unlit, took down his flute and began softly to play upon it.

The drummer and his wench stumbled out of the alcove, yawned, hiccupped, drained the last of the wine, bade the soldier a blurred good-night, and took their leave of him.

When he had heard them disappear tipsily out of earshot, the soldier took the blue flame from his knapsack in a corner of the room and lit his pipe. Out of the first curls of the grey smoke came the little demon, bowing and grimacing. He stood on the table at the soldier's side.

'Your will, master?'

'The same as last night. Let my servant come and clean up the room. It is not fit for a gentleman to sleep in.'

'Let *me* clean up the room, master. I can do it in no time.'

'Not you. It is woman's work. Bring hither the Princess.'

The manikin stopped grimacing, stood still, a look on his face of mingled alarm and admonition.

'There is danger, master. Have nothing to do with the Princess. The King and the court know of her disappearance last night.'

'Do they know where she went?'

'That they know not. But they are determined to find out if she leaves the palace again in her sleep. They have means.'

'I care not. Let her come.'

The little man pleaded and wheedled in vain.

'Very good, then. On your own head be it. I shall do my best to protect you. It is my duty. But I warn you. What you are doing is more dangerous than the field of battle. Courage will not help you.'

'No more words. If you are my servant, fetch here my other servant.'

The demon shrugged his little lean, naked shoulders, sprang into the air, and was gone.

As in a dream, not knowing whether it was the effects of the wine and the tobacco, the soldier once again beheld the Princess as she glided in at the open door. She stood before him, her eyes scarcely opened from sleep, her light robe wrapped closely about her slender body, her long hair dishevelled. In her face was no fear, but something of surprise and something of inner serenity, something of modest self-assurance.

The soldier, unsoftened by these appearances, said nothing, motioned with his head to the cupboard in which stood the broom. Just as before, the girl did her menial work, uncomplaining, competent, even cheerful.

'There is nothing a girl of good breeding does better,' the soldier said to himself as he watched her, 'than use a broom.'

Indeed, it was as if the Princess was unable to move without grace, whatever she did.

'Do you make no objection to this work, mistress?' the soldier said at length.

The girl stopped, rested her hands upon the top of the broom-handle, looked the soldier steadily in the face, smiling. Despite the smile, there was a tender sadness in her eyes which touched the soldier deeply. She said no word, only shook her head two or three times, slowly, from side to side.

'Are you dumb?'

The soldier spoke with a sudden sharpness, almost in anger.

'No.'

'Come here, girl.'

She obeyed, trailing the broom softly behind her.

'Look at me. Look at these clothes. Are they not fine? Tell me, mistress, could you fancy such a man as I for lover?'

'I am betrothed. I can fancy no man for lover, sir.'

Still she smiled. There was no rebuke in her tone. Her eyes were open now, as if full waking. In them was, it seemed to the soldier, a trace of mockery, a hint of amused disdain.

'But if you were *not* betrothed,' the soldier asked more urgently, 'if you were free?'

'How can I tell, sir? Truly – how can I tell?'

The first far chime of midnight broke in upon them. The girl paused a second or two, as if awaiting a signal of dismissal, and turned to replace the broom in the cupboard. Then, before the twelfth stroke had struck, the little demon came to conduct the Princess back to the castle. As before, he had taken the precaution of making himself invisible.

13. The Arrest

The children of the city long remembered the night it rained peas. First one child, then another, then whole groups of them made the discovery early next morning. The day was dry and fine, the streets were clean. At every corner there were to be had dried peas for the picking up – here a few, there a handful, until pockets were full, kerchiefs and aprons bulging with them. What laughter there was, what amazement, what incredulous merriment! Soon children from every quarter were running back to their mothers in the poorer districts, each with his little load of peas to be washed and made into soup or pudding.

Rising late, the soldier washed, put on his new clothes, went across the landing to the window in front of the inn to see what had brought the children out to scamper hither and thither over the square, laughing together, jostling like a flock of excited chicks, stooping to collect invisible somethings from the ground.

'It has been raining peas in the night. The whole city is strewn with dried peas. Manna in the wilderness, the priest says. Just look at the little ones! They've never seen anything like it. No more have I.'

The soldier sent the servant out for a screw of tobacco. Seated in his room, pipe in hand, he summoned the demon of the flame. The demon appeared, scowling – no grin, no bow this time.

'That was a narrow escape, master. You've led me a fine dance, and no mistake. But I warned you. Don't say I didn't warn you.'

'What are you talking about, and what's happened in town this morning? Has everyone gone mad?'

'You may well ask. That is my doing. Who scattered peas in alley, lane, street and square last night, if it wasn't I?'

'Stop talking gibberish and tell me what is wrong?'

'Yesterday morning the Princess's absence was noticed. She told the King she had had a dream. He suspected witchcraft and laid a plan to discover where she would go, if she were to disappear a second time. Master, I told you it wasn't safe to bring her here a second time.'

'She came and went without mishap, did she not? The King's daughter shall come as often as I choose. A fine gentleman like me needs his chambermaid, doesn't he?'

'I overheard them. I was in the palace when they told her to go to bed with the pocket of her robe full of dried peas. There was a hole in the pocket, so that the peas would show which way she had gone. It was a sorry device, but the palace sorcerer is a simple fellow, a bungler. A sorry device, but it might have worked. Do you see?'

The little black man appealed desperately to the soldier's bemused understanding.

'A trail of peas,' he went on, 'was to bring them to this door. Then they'd have discovered you. You'd have been for the rope, master.'

'Fiddlesticks! I've done her no harm. Besides, there are peas everywhere, it seems. Did she come with a cartload of them?'

'That was my doing. I put a stop to their game. First thing this morning, a carter came in from the country with a load of stuff – corn, raisins, twenty or thirty sacks of peas. He was a simple fellow, half-drunk and half-asleep. I led him about the town, this way and that. I slit his sacks, so that the peas strewed the streets like hailstones. There were peas at every house door, I tell you. The pigeons and the children have had the time of their lives. Their bellies are stretched like little drums.'

The soldier laughed and laughed, then complimented the manikin on his stratagem.

'That's all very fine,' answered the manikin, 'but no more dangerous games, do you hear? You'd best leave the girl alone, master. If you summon her again, I don't answer for the issue. For all I know, they're planning the next move at the palace now, even while you keep me talking here.'

'Well, get about your business, little fellow. Tonight she shall come again, just as usual. I'm not to be put off by fairy-tale tricks. I need my maidservant.'

The demon remonstrated furiously with his master, then shrugged his shoulders and vanished.

Nothing the demon had said discouraged him from his intentions. That evening, having dined and drunk alone, the soldier, relaxed, confident, summoned the little blackamoor and told him to fetch the Princess.

'I am here to obey. If the master wishes to destroy himself, none can prevent it. I have warned you to leave ill alone. The Devil knows what they have plotted at the palace this night to bring you to ruin.'

'If the Devil knows, then let the Devil protect me. Do as I say.'

'As you wish. But on your own rash head be it. If you will not listen to sense, then in the Devil's name be careful. The girl is soon to be married. They can't let this go on night after night, or there will be a scandal and the Count will cry off. They will do all in their power to find you out. I have tried to discover their minds but have failed. Only you can save yourself.'

Grumbling and querulous, the demon made off. The

soldier poured more wine, relit his pipe from a tinder-box, stretched himself at ease in a deep chair beside the table, brooding.

'What care I for threats? I was a soldier once. It is a strange revenge, but it is not displeasing. If I am in danger once more, what's that to me? Have I ever known what it is to be out of danger? I have served the King, and he has cast me off, unpaid, unthanked. Is it not right that his daughter shall serve me? ... And when I am tired of you, my dear, shall I not cast you off too?'

These last words were addressed to the Princess, who had at that moment appeared in the room. She made no sign of having heard him. Awaiting his command, she looked once more upon him as he sat at the table. The same dreamlike, untroubled look was in her face as she had worn before, the same inviolable serenity that had intrigued and yet irritated him.

'More wine.'

He indicated the wine-jug, and as she filled his glass, he looked intently into her face. There was still a faint mark or flush upon her cheek where his boot had struck her two nights before. It heightened rather than diminished her beauty in his eyes.

He drank, motioning her to the cupboard where the brushes were kept. Once more, patiently and competently, she swept and tidied his room. He followed her with his eyes, noting her unhurried grace, almost the grace of a dancer, not that of one performing a menial chore.

The soldier had a strong desire to talk with her, to make contact, but he did not know how to begin or what to say. She worked on, and he finished his wine. At last she had done sweeping and placed the broom back in the cupboard. Then she raised her hand to her mouth to hide a yawn.

'You're tired.'

'I am not used to doing without sleep.'

'Lie down over there – on my bed.'

Then the girl did an unexpected thing. Stepping over to a shelf, she took down the soldier's flute, placed it in his hands, looking at him as she did so, but saying nothing. When she had done this, she went into the alcove on the farther side of the room and stretched out on the bed. Had he turned, the soldier could have seen her as she lay half-hidden by the curtains. But he did not turn, remaining with his back to her. He raised the instrument to his lips, placed his fingers upon the holes as correctly as his maimed left hand would allow, blew a few notes, and then began to play. The tune was grave and slow, the old French song called 'L'amour de moy' that he had picked up somewhere on his campaigns. It was no soldier's song, no marching or drinking song, but now it seemed to suit his mood and the occasion. He had not played it for many years, and at first he stumbled and mistook the notes. At length he got it to his satisfaction, and the grave sweetness of the melody filled the room with its mournful cadences.

When the soldier had finished, he put down the flute and turned round.

The Princess lay as one asleep, her eyes closed, her mouth smiling as if in meditation. An overmastering desire not to wake the girl was harshly disturbed by the shrilling of the first cock.

The door swung open, blown by a sudden wind. At once the girl started up.

'Stay!' the soldier began, but already she was nearing the door, tugged by the demon's invisible hand.

'I cannot,' was all the Princess could say before she was drawn irresistibly away, and the door closed behind her.

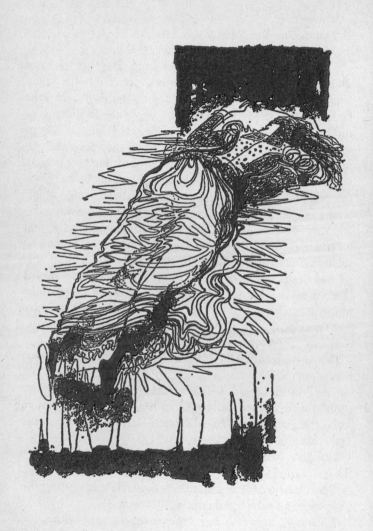

The soldier strode to the door and reopened it. The Princess was no longer to be seen. The soldier felt himself powerless to follow. He yawned, overcome by an unnatural weariness. There was nothing for him to do but throw off his finery and get into bed.

Beneath the bed, unknown alike to soldier and demon, was a slipper of white silk. The Princess had left it there by her father's order. She had not it in her to disobey him. To leave a sign of her presence in the place where she spent the night was the newest ruse of the palace counsellors. The trick with the peas had failed. This one might succeed.

It seemed as if the soldier had scarcely fallen asleep before he was awakened by a violent hissing at his ear and a tugging of his dark hair. The demon had come unsummoned, and was now, even before the city had fairly awoken, screaming at his master to rise and be gone.

'Get away from the city! The soldiers are out looking for you. They are calling at every inn in the place, knocking the landlord up in the King's name and ordering a search.'

'They'll not find me. How can they know –'

'Every stranger in the city will be hauled before the magistrates, and the Princess will be asked to name the man she has visited. They will stop at nothing. Master, master, have I ever disobeyed you? Do you owe me nothing? Who was it got you out of the witch's well? Do this one thing for me, I beg. Get out of here at once! Lose no time, I beg you.'

The soldier rubbed his eyes, pushed back his tousled hair, groped at the bed's foot for his breeches and doublet.

'I am still a soldier. I'll not run.'

'Fustian!' screamed the little imp. 'Any soldier of your age, if he be still living, has run a hundred times. There's a time for courage and a time for prudence.'

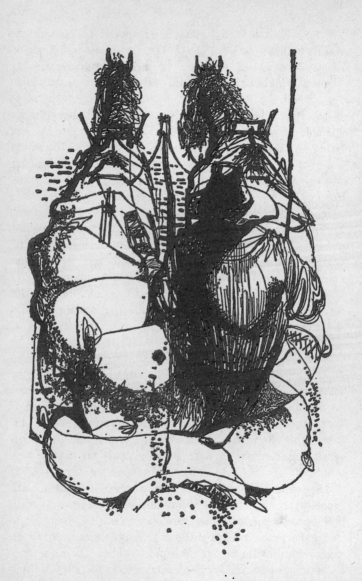

'Very well. But never forget that it is not among the least of your ill-doings that you have counselled me to cowardice.'

Hurriedly the soldier dressed, the demon dancing and gesturing about him. Suddenly a distant sound of shouting, followed by that of running boots. warned the soldier that he had no time to lose. Perhaps even now it was too late. Almost throwing himself down the stairs, he made his escape by a back door, as a squad of troopers tramped into 'The Wanton Child' by the front door.

The soldier enjoyed half an hour's freedom. It took the troopers but a few minutes to search the upper rooms and discover the silk slipper under the bed – a bed from which it was only too plain that someone had departed in haste. Roughly they questioned the landlord and the inn servants. The account of the soldier nearly enough answered to that given by the Princess to her father. They hurried from the inn, taking the landlord with them to identify his guest if they should find him.

The soldier was apprehended a furlong outside the city; he was climbing a gate into a field beyond which was the shelter of a wood. He made no resistance. He had left the inn with nothing but his clothes. Nor did he trouble to deny the charge of having abducted the Princess from the palace, three nights in succession, by strange means. The landlord identified him as the man who had occupied the room where the Princess's slipper had been found.

The soldier said little, scarcely protesting at his arrest. He did, however, instinctively look round to see if he might call upon the black imp for aid. But the imp was not to be seen, nor had the soldier the means to summon him. He had vanished the moment the approaching troopers were heard in the inn bedroom.

'I have done nothing,' the soldier said to himself, 'nothing amiss. They cannot say I have. And yet,' he added, repeating what he had said so often before, 'it is the end. I feel as if it is the end.'

He tramped between the troopers back into the city.

14. The Prison

Alone with himself in the prison, the soldier, cross-legged on his heap of musty straw, finished the wretched meal the warder had brought him. A bone and a crust remained. He flung them in a corner, stood up, stooping to avoid the low ceiling, stretched his limbs, lay down once more on the straw. Enough light came from the barred, unglazed window to show him the bare walls, stained and discoloured with the damps and growths of years, the scrawled heart-cries, the illiterate obscenities. The smell of rotting stone was mingled with the smells of human occupation. At first he had thought he might be left there till he fainted from starvation and died, forgotten, as he once imagined he might die in a different prison. But it seemed this was not to be his fate.

'You'll not be with us long, master, seemingly,' the sullen warder told him, leering from amidst the black stubble of his chin. 'You're for the courtroom tomorrow, they say. Short work they'll make of your trial, I shouldn't wonder. King's in a towering fit. Colloguing with the judges now, they say. I'd not be in your boots, master – fine as they are.'

'What am I charged with?'

'You know that as well as I do. Treason, they call it. Making off with the King's daughter like that. That's no way to go on, and her soon to be married.'

'That's not treason.'

'What you done is treason, master. No mistake. I hope, for your sake, the judge dines well tomorrow.'

'It's a lie. I committed no treason.'

'That's for them to say as knows, my fine gentleman.'

The food was rough but sufficient. The soldier dozed and drowsed on his straw. Little air came in from the small window; the afternoon sun, sending a shaft between the bars, warmed the atmosphere in the low, confined cell. A scratching and shuffling attracted his attention to a corner where a low, rusted grating separated the cell from some dark passage beyond. A grey-brown, furred creature as big as a small cat

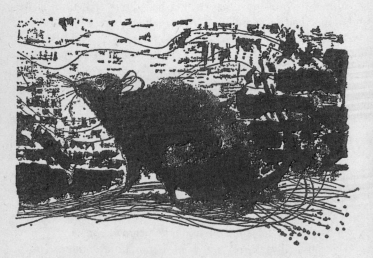

shuffled into the cell and made for the crust and bone discarded after the meal. Instinctively the soldier felt about himself for something to throw. But he had nothing. And why disturb the rat? It had done him no harm. He could not grudge it a share of his prison food. The button-eyes, bright, pointed teeth, and busy paws fascinated him.

'King Rat,' the soldier murmured, as the creature gnawed and nibbled on, 'eat your fill. Had I a dollar for you, you should have that too. I never served you five-and-twenty years; Your Majesty never turned me from your doors unthanked. Eat on, Your Majesty. Poor fare for a King, I fear.

I've known your father – your grandfather and great-grand-
father too, I dare say, and I bear them no ill-will. They were
my companions in the army – looking after their needs, mind-
ing their own affairs, owing no man more than a crust or a
bone.'

The rat gnawed on methodically, his ears cocked, his
shabby, long tail curled behind him.

'Only one thing I'd ask, Your Majesty. Have you such a
thing as a pipe of tobacco? It's all I crave.'

The visitor, abandoning the bare bone, made off behind the
grating. The sun crept round the wall, its barred square nar-
rowing and rising imperceptibly as the afternoon proceeded.
A sound of voices in the street outside – one of them familiar.
The soldier, his ears straining, got to his feet.

'Friend drummer!' he called. 'Hey, drummer, is that you?'

It was one of his companions at 'The Wanton Child'. For
a while the two talked in undertones through the window.
The soldier could scarcely see the face of his companion, so
high was the window above the level of the street. He could
not shout for fear of bringing the warder to his cell.

'I'd best not stay,' the drummer said. 'I'll be back. I'll get it
if it's to be found. Trust me.'

The barred rectangle of sunlight disappeared from the
corner of the cell. Daylight faded. No one came. But for a
passing murmur from the street, an occasional clatter of
hooves, the chiming of the city bells, there was no sound.
Sleep fell upon the prisoner fast in the Devil's arms, the
bosom of despair.

He was in a high hall, hung with the faded shows of her-
aldry. Subdued murmurs came from the close-packed throng.
On a great stage, overhung with a sombre, rich canopy, sat a
row of lawyer rats, gnawing quills. A rat in black, woman's
garments hung lifeless from a rafter over the stage. It had
the face of the witch who had imprisoned the soldier in the

well. On its head was perched a magpie, mumbling legal Latin. The soldier stood at the back of the hall, flanked by a guard of honour. All were rats. The hall was thronged with rats. A herald blew on a trumpet, and everyone was silent except for the bird aloft in the rafters. A grey, venerable figure stood up at one side of the stage and spoke. It was a voice the soldier had not heard before. It was dry and precise.

'You have served the kingdom of rats for five hundred years. You have toiled and marched, camped and battled in our cause, you have slain the witch who was the plague of us all.'

Thousands of button eyes glanced upwards at the hanging figure above the stage, and thousands of rat mouths grinned and leered.

'Approach, soldier! Let the soldier be brought forward. He shall be crowned King of the Rats. Your deeds have ennobled you, and you are henceforth styled "The Noble Rat"! Come and be crowned, Noble Rat, King of All Rats!'

At this there was a general clashing of little teeth and a sharp tapping of paw on paw, as the whole assembly applauded.

The guard of honour motioned the soldier forward, seizing him with their furred, angular hands. The soldier awoke, stiff and sweating. Instantly the dream ceased, and he jumped to his feet, striking his head on the ceiling. He had forgotten how low was his cell. He was conscious of a persistent tapping at the bars of his window.

'I've brought what you wanted. Here – take it. I mustn't be caught here.'

It was the voice of the drummer.

'I couldn't get into your room till late. It's watched. They're suspicious. But I got your bag.'

He could not push the soldier's knapsack through the narrow opening.

'Give me my pipe and tobacco, and that little pot with the light in it. It's all I need.'

The soldier waited. Then he saw the drummer's face dimly illuminated by a blue, flickering radiance. He took the light, then the tobacco-pipe and a paper of tobacco.

He thanked his friend, who departed hurriedly after bidding the soldier good-night and wishing him luck.

The soldier filled the pipe, applied the flame, drew in a mouthful of smoke, exhaled.

'Get me out of here, whether you are a devil or no.'

'That I cannot do,' the imp said ruefully. He was downcast and seemed even smaller, as if all the spirit had left him. 'These are strong walls, and yonder is a stout door with a good lock. You shall not go from here till the turnkey lets you out in the morning.'

'And then?'

'Then you will be guarded as you go to the hall of justice.'

'Justice!' the soldier said bitterly, pulling at his pipe.

In the darkness, though it was relieved by the blue light, the tobacco gave him small pleasure. But it was better than nothing.

'What do they know of justice?'

The demon shrugged his shoulders but said nothing.

'What care I?' groaned the soldier. 'If you can do nothing for me, there is no help in heaven or hell.'

'Be of good heart,' the demon said, 'the end is not yet. Be resolute, go to your trial, and be sure to have pipe, tobacco and light with you in your pockets. Come what may, let them not take these from you.'

'I will do as you say,' the soldier answered wearily. 'What else is there to do?'

'What indeed?'

Almost sprightly once more, the imp whirled his diminutive, naked body thrice round the soldier's head and made off on an unseen puff of smoke through the window.

The soldier finished smoking, knocked out the dottle, restored the charred pipe to his pocket. Then he rearranged his aching limbs and waited for morning.

15. The Trial

The gowned assessors sat at a long table, paper, ink and quills before them. Blue-jowled, black-browed or hook-nosed, some lean, some paunched, some with ruddy jowls agleam, others with yellow, pock-marked faces – they seemed collectively the embodiment and the guardians of injustice.

High on a dais behind them the bland King occupied the throne of justice. The Princess sat beside him, without colour or expression in her face. Armed guards flanked the pair. Below them, in the centre of the assessors, the judge sat, his clerk beside him. His face might have been a mask, wax and inhuman. It had no more reality than the wig that crowned it.

The throng that filled the hall of justice had been awed to silence by the command of court officials. Before, they had rumoured, swayed, pushed, a turbulent sea of inhumanity, greedy for disaster. The trial would be short. Justice would be done without delay. The Count in his neighbouring city was preparing to claim his bride, and there must be no scandal clinging to her name.

Alone in the dock, a guard on either side, the soldier stood, his face clenched and colourless. He wore his gentleman's clothes, which were all he had, but now they were soiled and awry from his handling in the prison.

'The end will be soon. Perhaps it has come already, and I am dreaming.'

There was no reality in the theatre tableau before his eyes – the beaked assessors, the stone judge, the King himself at the apex. Even the pale Princess was one whom he had never seen. She should have looked cold, disdainful, but of such a look she seemed incapable. As the proceedings began and the voices rose, fell, ceased and began again in question, answer, counter-question and explanation, the soldier's dream-sense increased. Even the advocate with whom the court had provided him was not real. Mechanically he said what was to be

said for the soldier, questioned the witnesses on his behalf, never turned once to speak to the man he was employed to defend. Accusation or defence, it was all one to him, a seasoned practitioner of law, committed to no interest in the issue of the proceedings.

It was a trial for treason, as such an occasion for the royal presence. The mute King was no more than a presence – a presence and a symbol. The Princess would be a witness when required.

On the witness-stand the landlord of 'The Wanton Child' testified to the soldier's good behaviour and sober conduct while under his roof. He knew nothing of the matter with which the soldier was charged, the abduction of Her Royal Highness on three several nights to perform menial tasks at the bidding of a common vagrant who had come by money enough to buy himself finery and good fare. How he had come by such money was not at issue, but the shrewd prosecutor used the question to create prejudice.

More than once the soldier was questioned.

'Does the prisoner deny that he abducted Her Royal Highness on three several occasions?'

'How could I abduct her? The palace is guarded. I had no men at command.'

'She came to the prisoner's room at her own will?'

'That question is not in order.'

'It may be answered.'

'I cannot tell.'

'For what purpose did the prisoner entertain Her Royal Highness in his room at night?'

'The floor needed to be swept, the dishes to be removed.'

Some smothered laughter and jeering was quelled by the court officials.

'I beg leave to call Her Royal Highness.'

'She may answer your questions from where she sits.'

'Very good.'

The soldier's advocate raised his eyes to the slight figure on the dais, spoke clearly, throwing his voice up to the extremity of the high chamber.

'Does Her Royal Highness deny the matters that have been testified to?'

She shook her head.

'Did Your Highness go of your own free will?'

Expectancy moved the thronged hearers.

'I hardly know. I felt constrained, but by what or whom I cannot tell.'

'Did Your Highness object to the conduct of the prisoner?'

'No.'

'What violence or unseemliness did he offer?'

'None that I recall.'

The prosecutor rose swiftly.

'It has been testified by servants at the palace that there was a mark or bruise upon Your Highness's cheek after the first occasion when Your Highness was constrained to visit the prisoner. Can you tell the court how it came there?'

'I cannot. Nor can it have been severe, for that was but three days ago, and my mirror testifies that it is there no longer.'

The Princess's reply was clear, firm and unequivocal, the mere recital of a fact, but it pleased the more thoughtful of the crowd.

The proceedings, that had begun to seem interminable to the soldier in his dream-state, now accelerated and came abruptly almost to their conclusion. The prosecutor once more alleged the soldier's unquestionable guilt and called for the severest penalty which the crime of high treason could incur. All knew it was death. The advocate for the prisoner summed up, formally and without emotion, the reasons for clemency. It was now the turn of the bench of assessors. They nodded, mumbled, ejaculated, argued, gestured. In their midst the judge sat cold and unconcerned, fidgeting languidly at his fingernails with the point of a quill. His clerk scratched at a paper, sniffing. The crowd murmured incessantly under the disapproving gaze of the court officials, silencing them with their eyes. The soldier seemed at length to have awoken from a sleep. His face was a mask that spelt an agony of anxiety. Never had he needed more his now almost habitual sardonic self-control, his dedication to the virtue of despair. At last the end of the trial was in view. There was movement among the assessors, a stirring of pens as a paper was passed down the line. Marks were made beside the names. No one could see them beyond the assessors' bench. The paper was handed to the judge, who motioned it to his clerk, ignoring it. The clerk studied it, sniffed, muttered sibilantly to his master through the piled wig. Then the judge stood up. The court was silenced. All gazed at the stone man, statue of law and power. Never had a voice been colder. It was a voice that brought to the least receptive mind the image of a mortuary. It was as if he had risen from the dead to speak, and his tone chilled the very walls of the sepulchre.

'Your Majesty. You have heard the facts of this case. Between defence and prosecution they are common ground. The actions performed by the accused, as witnessed before this court and not denied by the accused, are base and beyond belief. The dignity of the royal house has been struck at, the honour of the Princess impugned.'

('He's for the gallows,' spoke the minds of the people.)

'The circumstances of this action are in question, the motive uncertain, the means not known. But of the facts there is no question.'

('First he will be put to torture, till he screams for death.')

'Nevertheless —'

('What now?')

'– we must bear in mind the crime of which the prisoner is accused. Treason – high treason – is the basest of crimes, threatening as it does the very foundations of the state. No one denies this. Yet the evidence for high treason as adduced by the prosecution is insufficient. Unthinkable, as this man's crime is, I cannot find that it constitutes anything defined by our law as treason.'

(A sudden gasp of amazement. The stone oracle had spoken the altogether unexpected.

'He will be flogged, flogged and set free. He will be imprisoned for life, but not hanged.')

But the statue still stood. The voice had not ceased. The soldier, torn by a conflict of relief and anxiety, gazed steadfastly into the judge's face. The voice rose, quickened a fraction, took on a less chilly resonance.

A murmur in the crowd was quickly stifled.

'This charge is false. There can be no question of high treason. To call this man's actions by that name would be to make a mockery of this court and of our law.'

Still the judge had not finished. He raised his hand, the first gesture he had yet made, to still the rising breath of the stupefied audience.

'That, however, is not what matters.'

He was no longer a statue, his voice came no more from the tomb but from the breast of a living man.

'What matters in a case of this kind,' (his voice now was thunder) 'is the safety and dignity of majesty. That the agents of the law have bungled their submission is of no import whatever. I am here to uphold the dignity and propriety of majesty, which has been affronted beyond repair.' (Now he was sweating. His voice rose terribly, like the wind of a storm.) 'The technicalities of the law, the niceties of legal and juristic definition, are mere toys. What we have to deal with is not play-acting but life. Life and death. You –'

(thundering directly at the soldier) '– are guilty beyond re-
demption. You are sentenced to summary execution. That is
the judgement of this court. It is irrevocable. Soldiers, take
him away and hang him. Do your duty. Long live the
King!'

16. The Reckoning

The court was in turmoil. Save for the judge, who subsided into his chair, overcome by exhaustion, everyone stood up. There were cries of 'Traitor! Hang him! No, let him have justice! Whip the traitor! The law on the judge! A reprieve: where is justice?' In the uproar, no one heard the Princess's gasp of incredulous dismay. She turned to her father, but the King ignored her, shook off her hand, stepped forward, raised his arm in authority. The prisoner's guards had seized him roughly by his two arms. Court officials were quelling the crowd with words and blows. Then all saw the King's upraised hand. There was silence as he spoke, directly to the prisoner, quietly.

'You have heard the sentence of the court. There is no appeal. The law is above us all, even above Kings. Have you anything to say? Stand back, guards. Let him speak if he wishes.'

The King was bland, authoritative, almost smiling. The soldier, gasping and choking with indignation, released from the grasp of his guards, ripped open his jacket, tore it off, flung it down before him, burst from his shirt and revealed his scarred and heaving chest. There was a tense and horrified silence.

'I served you in war. Look at my wounds. Twenty-five wounds, twenty-five years. If I am to die, I will die with my scars in the sight of all!'

His voice was hysterical. He tried to tear off the rest of his clothes, but the guards seized him once more, and he yielded,

panting and sobbing. Only the soldier's panting and sobbing
broke the frozen stillness of the hall.

'Enough of this.'

The King had lost a shade of his blandness.

'Past services do not condone present crimes. One arm of
the state is its soldiers. The other, and the higher, is the law.
You are to be hanged. Before that is done, prisoner, have you
a last request? The law is hard, but I am not unmerciful.'

The soldier's paroxysms had almost ceased while the King
spoke. He was now quiet. He said nothing.

'Come, prisoner, your last wish. O draught of wine – a
farewell to some friend.'

The soldier was calm. Through the tears still standing in his eyes, some might have fancied he smiled.

'Then, if you have no last wish, will you not ask my daughter's pardon for the insults you have given her?'

'I have given no insult,' the soldier said firmly, 'and she would not wish me to ask her pardon. She knows I bade her do nothing unbecoming a woman, a modest woman. No. That I will not do. But a last request I have.'

'Good. Name it, prisoner.'

The crowd listened in surprise.

'Give it him, father. Let him have it, whatever it may be.'

The voice of the Princess was heard throughout the hall. 'Name it.'

'It has nothing to do with your daughter. I ask only one thing: to be allowed to smoke a last pipe of tobacco in this courtroom.'

There was a murmur almost of amusement at such a trivial request. Yet, the old soldiers in the hall reflected, this was a natural enough request for a man under sentence of death. The crowd's amusement was too much for the Princess. Weeping softly, she buried her face in her hands and ran out of the hall, followed by her maid.

The King was smiling broadly.

'By all means,' he agreed. 'Two pipes, if you wish, prisoner. I am not a hard man.'

'One will be enough.'

Swiftly he picked up his jacket, fumbled in the pockets, drew out his pipe and tobacco, prepared to light up. Before it was clear, even to those nearest him, what was happening, he took the little jar from another pocket and held the flickering blue flame to the pipe's bowl. As the smoke rose, a cloudy wisp of violet, in the air of the hall, the demon materialized and perched on his master's shoulder. His eyes cracked with excited malevolence, each of his few inches charged with superabundant energy. There was no bowing and grinning. Instead, the demon held in his hand a tiny sword of flashing blue metal, its point sharp as a needle. Those near enough to see clearly the naked manikin crossed themselves, shrank away from something so manifestly possessed by supernatural potency.

'Help me now!' cried the soldier. 'I'll not die for any King on earth, or his judge straight from hell!'

This reanimated the judge, who roared back:

'You shall be flogged for this before you hang! Take him and strip him, men-at-arms, I say!'

But the demon was too quick. Cutting and jabbing furiously with his small, wicked sword, he flew straight at the judge. The judge dropped to the floor as if hewn by an axe. He was stone dead. Hissing and screaming exultantly, the demon laid about him on all sides. Wherever he struck, there was death. The assessors, clawing at each other to get away, fell in heaps. Among the armed men and the court officials there was a huge slaughter. The crowd screamed, jammed the doors. Some tried to cut the black manikin to pieces with sword or dagger, but they had no power over him. At last all who had not been able to get out of the hall knelt or lay on the floor, shielding their heads from the fury of the soldier's guardian and avenger.

The King, struggling down from his dais amidst the terrified throng, had stumbled and fallen. Now he knelt at the assessors' table, gibbering with fear and white as the scattered leaves scrawled by the clerks of the court. Above him, on the table, the demon exulted, his sooty skin glistening with sweat, his small chest heaving, his bloody weapon shining darkly within inches of the King's face. Behind him the soldier looked on. He had put on his jacket once again, more for protection than to hide his nakedness. Round the three of them

the dead lay in heaps, the wounded groaned, some crawled and slunk to the doors. The furious imp was master of all.

'Spare my life, soldier,' the King begged. 'Spare my life, for the sake of my child.'

'You are condemned to die,' the soldier said triumphantly. 'This is justice, and against justice there is no appeal.'

'What crime have I committed?'

The King whined as he pleaded, his face distorted with terror.

'The crime of degrading the royal dignity, the crime of appointing corrupt justices. A fig for law! To kill you would be justice.'

'Ask him what he will give in exchange for his life,' the demon said. 'It will do you no good to kill him.'

'True. King, answer my servant's question. What will you give for your life?'

'I will give you one of the two things I hold most precious.'

The King had recovered something of his composure, now that his fear of instant death was allayed.

'What are those?'

'My kingdom or my daughter.'

The soldier paused, sighing. Then he spoke.

'Your daughter is promised to another. You cannot give her twice, even to save your life. I will take your crown. I will not make a royal king, but I will try to be a just one. There is much wrong in your kingdom. You shall help me to right it.'

'So be it.'

The King had already risen to his feet.

'I say this in the presence of all who still live and hear me. Henceforth this man shall wear my crown. Obey him and commit no treason. Men-at-arms, those who are left, take up your weapons again and lay them at this man's feet. That is

my last order. You are now under his command, to die for
him if need be.'

Some half-dozen men-at-arms did as they were bidden. The
soldier constituted them his bodyguard, bade them conduct
him to the palace. The demon had disappeared. The blue light
was stowed safely in the new King's pocket.

7. The Choice

From the top of the steep edge surmounted by the castle and the palace the soldier gazed out over the country of which he was King. Late afternoon sunshine varnished the far fields, roads, houses, treetops in a golden glow. He was alone. He sat on a low stone wall beneath which a steep and bushy slope overhung the moat curling close about the castle hill. Idly he picked up a small round stone from the gravel behind him and tossed it over the edge. Seconds later he heard it strike the surface of the water with a tiny click. He was aware of a passing impulse to leap the low wall and himself plunge into the moat. It was no more than an impulse, which he rejected without even a shudder.

Behind him, across the broad breadth of the mound, the outer walls of the castle showed black against the setting sun. There was no one in sight. Within the castle the servants would be going about their usual business. In the afternoon he had seen stewards and chamberlains on official business which it was only too clear they understood and he did not. Yet on the whole they had been kind. They were not averse to a change, and they knew the wisdom of making the right impression of capable servility on their new master. It was the master himself who was inwardly ill at ease, uncertain of the rightness of what he had done, unconvinced of his own aptitude for his wholly novel and unexpected situation.

As he gazed over the countryside before him, it was as if to put behind him the thought of palace life and intrigue, with all that it held to frighten and distress him; it was as if he found greater assurance in contemplating the life of

farmers and foresters, soldiers and wayfarers, the people of his
country, the people to whom he belonged and whose lot he
would surely do what he could to lighten. A wagon drawn
by two horses was just visible toiling away into the distance
along the white road leading eastwards from the city. Rooks
were beginning to gather among the treetops. A distant
weathercock caught the gleam of the nearly level sun. A
patch of white dust appeared from the shadow of the hill
beneath the soldier and moved rapidly along the road. The
sound of hooves at the gallop betrayed a solitary rider making away from the city at speed. A messenger, doubtless,
anxious not to be overtaken by night before reaching his
goal.

'What in the world am I doing here?' the soldier asked
himself.

Deep inside him was the conviction that he had made the
wrong choice, that he had always made the wrong choice. As
a boy he had chosen the wrong trade; he should have stuck to
farming, like his father and his brothers. And now, that very
morning, he had again made the wrong choice. Any man of
sense in his situation would have taken the Princess and left
the King his crown and the burdens of kingship. True, she
was betrothed to another; nor had he wished, if the truth were
told, to get a bride by such extraordinary means as were then
presented to him. He had already come to the conclusion that
he had no ambition to rule the kingdom. One thing and one
thing only stood between him and the immediate and defini-
tive abdication he had been contemplating: the desire to
do justice to poor undefended men, soldiers and citizens,
beggars and homeless ones, labourers without land, poor
folks in the grip of hard masters and bad laws. This was
surely enough; this would give him plenty to live and work
for.

The soldier felt the need of counsel. Tomorrow he would

call together the best of his advisers. For the present, however,
another plan occurred to him. He felt in his pockets, drew
out pipe, tobacco and flame. It was still there, flickering coolly
in the little earthenware pot. He could at least seek advice
from his supernatural counsellor and protector. After stuffing
the charred bowl of the tobacco-pipe, he was about to apply
the flame when he was startled by a light sound behind him, a
sudden footstep on the gravel. The little pot escaped from his
hand, struck the top of the wall on which he was sitting,
bounced clear of the bushes, dropped irrecoverably into the
waters of the moat. There was a splash, and the soldier could
just make out a widening ripple as the water closed over the
tiny flame. He had no time to wonder if his demon would
ever reappear, no time to feel panic or even discomfiture at
the sudden loss of what had been his solace and salvation.
The Princess was standing beside him, begging his pardon for
having startled him.

'It is no matter.'

The soldier rose, put away his pipe, spread on the wall the
short cloak he had been wearing about his shoulders. He
motioned her to sit, then seated himself once more. For a
long time they sat silent, looking over the darkening
landscape.

'I am glad to see you once more before you go, so that I may
beg your pardon.'

'For what, Your Majesty?'

The girl spoke quietly, gravely, without mockery.

'I shall not be Your Majesty when you have gone to marry
the Count. But I shall be happier if I may have your pardon
for the wrong I did you.'

'It was no wrong. The work you made me do was not un-
worthy of any who knows herself a woman. It did not dis-
please me.'

'Then perhaps you can forgive me for taking your father's

kingdom. I suppose he will go to live with you and the Count.'

The Princess said nothing.

'Do you care for the Count?'

'I hardly know him. I had rather not speak of him.'

It was the soldier's turn to be silent.

The Princess spoke again.

'My father would have been a better King if my mother had lived. Do not think too badly of him. It saddened him, and made him hard. It made him colder than he is by nature. He was not a kind King, but he was not a wicked one.'

'I shall be a bad King. I wish I had him to help me. Once a King, always a King. Once a soldier, always a soldier. In lands where I have been, soldiers have not seemed to me to make good kings. It seems to me that I shall always make wrong decisions. I believe I made a wrong decision today.'

The Princess said nothing, but continued to look at the soldier as he sat beside her. He was troubled, she smiling sadly.

'Well, there is much to do, many wrongs to right, many debts to pay.'

'Debts?'

'Yes. Much is owing to my soldiers, to begin with. A King needs a contented army. That at least I know.'

'Will you be at war?'

'Who knows? At all events, no country can be at peace where old soldiers roam the land as beggars.'

The soldier spoke with indignation. The Princess looked down at her companion's maimed left hand as it rested on the parapet beside her.

'You suffered much for my father. I wish you well as king – truly and sincerely I do. Perhaps you will one day be at war with the Count. Then what would you do?'

The soldier laughed, a deep-chested, soldier's laugh, and slapped his thigh with his right hand.

'Perhaps I shall march on your country, kill the Count and seize you for my wife. I shall need a Queen. You are the only Queen I could fancy. I might have had you as a gift from your father. I chose wrong this morning. But how could I take you as the price of your father's life? How could I take you when you were betrothed to another?'

'And if I were not?'

The Princess spoke coolly, seriously, requiring an answer.

'Then I would ask for your hand. Indeed, if I were not a fool and a simpleton, as I have been my life long, I would have taken you and left the kingdom to your father, let the Count do what he would. But once a soldier, always a soldier. Once a fool, always a fool. I cannot take a gentlewoman by force. That, I dare say, is the height of folly.'

'Perhaps . . . perhaps not. But if you had, you would never have known if I could care for you. A soldier may be proud as well as foolish. Besides, have you not work to do as King?'

'I might have done it as heir to the throne. But now I must do it alone, without your help, without your father's help. You go to live with the Count. I stay to rule the country, for better or for worse.'

'Yes, indeed, soldier, you are foolish – proud and foolish. If you chose wrongly today, who knows but that you will always choose wrongly? Oh, you are stupid – stupid !'

Overcome by this sudden outburst, which had astonished herself as much as the soldier, the Princess buried her face in her hands and rose from the wall, stumbling blindly away towards the dark bulk of the palace. At that moment her father appeared. He caught her in his arms as she came towards him. Together they returned to the soldier, now on his feet.

The former King spoke rapidly, formally.

'Your Majesty,' he said deliberately, 'I come to ask for your protection, for asylum in the kingdom for a time. Doubtless my daughter has been telling you of our plight. Has she asked for asylum for herself and me? If so, have you granted it?'

'No,' the soldier replied without comprehension. 'I know nothing of asylum. She has asked no favour.'

'Then you know nothing of our plight. I will tell you, so that you shall know why it is necessary for me to throw myself and my daughter on your mercy.'

The King spoke rapidly, precisely. The Princess looked neither at him nor at the soldier.

'The Count's envoy was present at our proceedings this morning. No sooner were they concluded than he rode post-haste to his master and informed him of what had gone on. The Count, who is a resolute and impetuous man, instantly sent word to the palace that, since I had no longer possession of the kingdom and my daughter, his betrothed, would not succeed to it on my death, he regarded the match as at an end. We were to have travelled this evening to his country and taken up residence with him. I could not stay a day longer in the kingdom I have lost. This news came while my daughter and I were making preparations to leave. But you knew nothing of this? Has my daughter told you nothing? I had hoped she was prevailing upon you to let us stay here for the time being.'

The King awaited an answer from the astonished soldier. The Princess, now calm, said nothing.

At last the soldier spoke.

'You may stay. Of course you may stay – as long as you choose. I shall have need of advice. Please go in and give orders that you are to remain in your present quarters. The Princess and I will follow you.'

In the little daylight that was left the soldier could not see the King's expression, but he was aware of the other's relief. The Princess stood beside him, watching her father's departure. Then she turned and looked at the soldier, searching the darkness to read the puzzled expression on his scarred face.

For a long time he said nothing. She shivered slightly. He took his cloak from the wall, shook it out, placed it round her shoulders. Her fingers went up to touch lightly the back of his maimed left hand. He spoke.

'So you knew of this already, Your Highness – this behaviour of the Count. Tell me of it. Tell me, I beg.'

'I had rather not talk of it,' the Princess said. 'You heard what my father said. That is all. I had rather not talk at all. I would like to go indoors. It is getting cold.'

Slowly he led her towards the palace, his hand still resting on her shoulder.

'I had rather hear you play on your flute. Perhaps you would do that for me.'

Some other Puffins you might enjoy

THE WEATHERMONGER

Peter Dickinson

A story about England in the future. But instead of
everything being *more* civilised, something has gone
wrong and we are back in the middle ages. Geoffrey and
Sally find the origin of the magic, and because Sally is
good at Oral Latin they destroy it and restore England
to its modern self.

I AM DAVID

Anne Holm

David lay quite still in the darkness of the concentration
camp, waiting for the signal. 'You must get away
tonight,' the man had told him. 'Stay awake so that
you're ready just before the guard is changed. When
you see me strike a match, the current will be cut off and
you can climb over – you'll have half a minute, no more.
Follow the compass southwards till you get to Salonica
and then find a ship that's bound for Italy, and then
go north till you come to a country called Denmark –
you'll be safe there.'

So David, who had known no other life but that of the
concentration camp, escaped into a world he knew
nothing of, not even what things to eat nor how to tell
good men from bad.

A deeply moving story, highly recommended for readers
of 11 and over.

GINGER OVER THE WALL

Prudence Andrew

There were four boys in the gang, Toni Reynolds, Tiny Thomas, Andy Martin and Ginger Jenkins. Ginger was the leader, and they had a good headquarters in a pigeon loft behind Toni's house, safe from Bert Hughes and his band of toughs.

Then the pigeon loft burnt down, and Ginger's lot found another place. But a real adventure came along, a big and frightening one – they got mixed up in a real crime and came near to disaster by hiding an innocent man from the police. Or was their friend Carlo as innocent as he said?

THE STARLIGHT BARKING

Dodie Smith

Pongo and Missis, the famous pair in *The Hundred and One Dalmatians*, wake up one morning to discover that every living thing is in a deep sleep – except the dogs. And this is only the beginning of some very strange happenings.

If you have enjoyed this book and would like to know about others which we publish, why not join the Puffin Club? Membership costs 10s. a year for readers living in the U.K. or the Republic of Ireland, (15s. in European countries, 25s. elsewhere) and for this you will be sent the Club magazine Puffin Post four times a year and a smart badge and membership card. You will also be able to enter all the competitions. There is an application form overleaf.

APPLICATION FOR MEMBERSHIP OF THE PUFFIN CLUB

(Write clearly in block letters)

To: The Puffin Club Secretary,
Penguin Books Ltd,
Harmondsworth, Middlesex

I would like to join the Puffin Club. I enclose my membership fee for one year (see below) and would be glad if you would send me my badge and copy of *Puffin Post*.

Surname ....

Christian name(s)...

Full Address...

....

....

Age.................Date of Birth.............................

School (name and address).................................

....

Where I buy my Puffins ....

Signature (optional)........................... Date...........

Note: Membership fees for readers living in:
The U.K. or the Republic of Ireland   10s.
European countries   15s.
Elsewhere   25s.